# Chapter 1

Katie and Jase finally began to feel safe once more.
They ended up moving up to the cabin, owned by Jase,
up in the Rocky Mountains. That was when Jase first
realized that he was in love with Katie. He never knew
that he would soon have a family. Michael enjoyed it
there. He was getting to know his, Aunt Rebecca and
Uncle Derek. Athina was a good baby. She would sleep
most of the night and hardly cried.

Sadie and Jackson had a little girl, that they named
Anna. They had moved to California for business. Jase
would fly them in for a visit anytime they wanted or
were able to. They were still very much in love and had
a good life.

Jessica was still believed to be dead, so they felt
everything was okay. No one was out to get them. Katie
would often talk about, Dylan. They never told Michael
that Dylan was his real father. It would be too confusing
and probably too much to handle. He had already gone
through so much.

Jase continued working from home until Katie felt safe
again. It was nice being around her every day. He could
sit and stare at her all day. She was as beautiful to him
today as she was when he first saw her. She almost
looked like an angel. Her hair was dark and wavy,
perfect for him to grab, while he kissed her wildly
passionate. Her lips were soft and gentle. When she
would walk by he would get a glimpse of her perfume. It
would remind him of being out in a field of flowers in
the springtime air. He often studied her body. The way

she would walk or bend over in front of him. She was a distraction, that he couldn't get enough of. His mind would wander from work and picture bending her over his desk and pulling her arms behind her back, while he pounded her warm, tight, wet hole. It took all he had to contain himself.

Katie walked into the room. She could tell that Jase was deep in thought, so she didn't want to disturb him. She stood in the doorway admiring him from afar. He was the perfect man. Not only gorgeous and nice to look at, but he was the greatest father that she could have given her children. He knew just how to love her. He was so sexy hot with that chiseled body of his and that rigid jawline. She loved nibbling his neck and running her fingers through his hair. What she wouldn't give to let him have his way with her on that desk.

She snapped out of her sexual fantasy when Jase called her name. "Hey, Beautiful! Are you ok?" He worried.

She cleared her throat and fanned herself with her hand. "Yes, Sorry. I was in my own little world."

He just smiled at her and then looked at her from head to toe. "You look rather sexy this morning."

She blushed because she knew he was lying. She had just got the baby down for a nap and was in her nightgown with bags under her eyes. She had to look like a frightful mess. "You are lying or blind?" She giggled as she tried to fix her hair.

Jase got up and walked over to her. He tucked her hair behind her ears. "Don't do that."

"Do what?" She looked down at her messy sleeping attire.

"You are beautiful to me, when you are dressed to go out, or when you are dressed like this. I see you, not what you wear. I love every inch of you. You never have to be a shame of how you look."

She blushed. "I know you fell in love with me before I had children and looked like a mom."

He lifted her chin to meet her gaze. Those soft green eyes, so full of shame. "Honey, you are most beautiful to me now. I can't stop thinking about you."

She smiled up at him. "You always know just what to say."

He had an idea. "How about, we ask Rebecca to keep the kids this weekend. Then you and I can have a romantic weekend. Just the two of us?" He proposed.

She liked the sound of that. "That would be nice. Maybe rent a movie and cuddle on the couch?"

He leaned in and kissed her softly. "Or I could make love to my beautiful wife, that is driving me insane right now."

She felt warm and tingly all over. Was he thinking the same as her? Was he also lusting for her?

"I miss your touch." She informed him. "It just seems so hard for us to connect... sexually."

"I know and I am sorry. We will get better about it." He kissed the tip of her nose.

She smiled at him. She got to see the side of him that she had missed. Having children made it difficult for them to make love. Most of the time, it had been short and sweet because they didn't know when Michael or Athina would interrupt them.

"It is still nice all the times that we make love, but sometimes I just want a little more." She admitted.

"Like what?" He tried to get her to confess what she desired.

She pushed him back jokingly. She was always too shy to talk dirty, and he knew it but loved seeing her blush. She went to walk away and Jase grabbed her by the arm and pushed her against the wall. He gave her the most passionate kiss that he had given her in a long time.

She mind was spinning and her body was aching. She had longed for his touch and it felt good. His big, strong hands were on her breasts as he continued kissing her. It was wild, erotic, and sent pleasure throughout her body. He took her bottom lip and bit down gently making her cry out with delight.111S3E3E He then tugged her hair back, causing her to arch her head and he nibbled on her neck. The warmth of his breath against her skin sent chills down her body. He quickly shut the door beside them, lifted her nightgown, and pulled her panties off. He grabbed her leg and pushed it up as he pulled his jeans from his body. He slid himself inside of her. The pleasure was intense. She dug her nails into his back and moaned.  He thrashed harder and deeper inside of her. He ached for this. He needed to be inside of her. This time he would not take no for an answer. He wanted to devour every inch of her body. Their bodies rocked even harder until he exploded with pleasure inside of her. Her leg dropped to the floor and he held her against the wall with his body. He caressed his face in her hair and nuzzled her cheek with his nose. "That is just the beginning."

The sound of his voice against her ear could turn her on just as fast as his touch. "Thank you." She smiled at him.

"No... Thank you, Beautiful." He kissed her lips once more before pulling his jeans up.

Katie pulled herself together. "I am going to take a quick bath before, Athina, wakes up. I won't belong."

"Take your time. I will take care of her while you are bathing." He assures her.

She winked as she slips away out of his office. He smiled as he watched her walk away. He could see her sexy legs were shaky from the pleasure he gave her and he loved every bit of it.

Athina was crying. She had just woken up and Jase
went to get her. He lifted her from her crib. "Hey there
my sweet little girl." He nestled her against his chest
and kissed her little nose. "Daddy's here."

She stopped crying when she heard his voice. She
looked up at him with her big green eyes. She looked so
much like Katie. "What is it? Did you miss Daddy?"

She just studied his facial expression. All of a sudden,
Jase smelled something. "P...U... I don't think you
missed me. I think you just needed a clean diaper." He
chuckled under his breath. "Let's get you cleaned up."

He brought her over to the changing table and laid her
down. He cleaned her up and got her dressed. "You are
the most beautiful, bald little girl I know." He lifted her
into his arms and kissed her cheek. "Daddy loves you
and your brother, very much. You guys are my whole
world."

A knock came at the door and distracted, Jase from
spending time with his daughter. He carried her
downstairs and answered the door.

"Surprise!" It was Rebecca and Derek.

They had balloons and gifts for the baby and Michael.

"Oh my goodness... Is this Athina?" Rebecca asked.

Jase couldn't resist. "No this is some baby we stole
from the neighbor last night." He laughed.

Rebecca pushed him softly. "Shut up, you know what I
meant." She giggled.

Jase held the door and had them come inside. He
handed the baby to Rebecca and went upstairs to let
Katie know that they had guests.

When Katie and Jase returned, Rebecca and Derek
were sitting on the couch cuddling with the baby.
Rebecca loved babies and she would make a great Aunt.
She was going to spoil the kids to death.

"I am so sorry, that we haven't come around sooner."
Rebecca apologized.

"Don't be sorry. We all have crazy lives right now."
Katie spoke up.

"I have to get Michael in a little while. Derek? Would
you like to ride with me?" Jase asked him when he saw
the time.

"Sure, sounds great." He agreed.

Jase and Derek kissed their wives and headed out the
door.

Rebecca and Katie sat idol with the baby.  Rebecca was
in love with being an Aunt. She couldn't get enough of
seeing her adorable little face. "She looks just like you."

Katie grinned. "That's what Jase says as well, but I think
she is even more beautiful."

"Yeah, we always think our children are more beautiful
than any other being in this world." Rebecca noticed
that Katie seemed a  little down. "Is everything ok,
honey?"

Katie sighed and began to open up. "It's just Jase seems
so distant right now. I feel like something is going on,
but he will not open up to me."

Rebecca just listened.

"I mean sex is great when the kids are asleep or away,
but I feel like he is a closed book. Do you know if he is
keeping something from me?"

"Katie, that is a conversation that you should have with
your husband. If he has something to share, he would
tell you." Rebecca stood up and rocked the baby in her
arms.

"I just feel like I don't know enough about him. Every
time I ask about his family history, he shuts me out."
Katie watched Rebecca become antsy.

"Katie, you need to talk to Jase. I am sure everything is
fine and that he will come around soon."

"So there is something? What is going on? Why the big
secret?" Katie grew suspicious.

"Listen, this is not for me to disclose, but yes,
something did happen in our childhood. Something
terrible and when Jase decides to talk about it, he will.
He just has to do it on his own. You are his wife and I
can't be the one to tell you."

Katie was even more nervous now, knowing that her
husband had a secret.

"Listen, Katie, it is nothing that will alter the way he
feels about you. We all have secrets. That is how
relationships grow. We slowly, but surely learn them all
and then love each other more because of them. I am
sure he will open up to you soon."

Katie frowned. The answer is not what she wanted, but
she knew not to press too much. "Ok, you're right. I am
sorry for putting you on the spot."

"It's fine. I know it is hard to love someone that has
secrets, but his secret is nothing that concerns you. It is
just something we swore to never talk about. But Derek
knows and I am sure that Jase will tell you soon. Just be
patient."

Rebecca handed the baby to Katie. "I have to run to the
restroom. I will be right back."

Jase and Derek pulled up at the school. Michael came
running to the car when he saw Derek. He was so
excited to see his uncle in the car. "Daddy? Did you
bring Athina?"

"No, she stayed home this time. Aunt Rebecca wanted
to spend time with her." Jase answered. "Buckle up and
we will stop for ice cream on the way home."

"Yay!" Michael grew excited and buckled his seatbelt as
they drove away.

Jase began to open up to Derek. Through the years the two of them had become more like brothers.

"I am thinking about telling Katie about our family." He started.

Derek glanced over at him. "Are you sure? I mean, I think it is great if you do, but I know you have a hard time talking about it."

"I know and I do not want to bring her into this, but we were kids. I am sure she would understand."

"That is exactly what your sister has been telling you."

Jase rolled his eyes. "I know, but I had to make sure it was right."

"Jase, that lady loves you. I think she would be the best one to help you through this."

"Yeah, me too man." Jase pulled into the ice cream shop parking lot.

"Yay! Ice cream!" Michael hollered out in the backseat.

The men laughed at his excitement. They ordered their ice cream and headed back to see their wives. Michael was enjoying his ice cream and singing along to the radio, when out of nowhere, a truck slammed into the side of their car, sending them spinning in circles. Jase smashed his head on the steering wheel, Derek was knocked unconscious with his bleeding against the window, and Michael was passed out from hitting his head against the door of the car.

When they woke up, all three of them were in the hospital. Katie and Rebecca were standing over them. "Hey." Katie rested her hand on Jase's knee.

"What happened?" Jase was groggy.

"Relax, you were in a wreck." She responded.

"Michael?" He cried.

"Michael is fine. He is on the pediatric floor. He barely has a scratch. Derek is in the bed behind that curtain. Everything is fine."

"Did the guy that hit us, make it?"

"Unfortunately, whoever it was, ran off. The truck was stolen and they have no idea who it was. It was a hit and run."

Jase clenched his fist. He became angry, that someone almost killed his son.

"Honey, calm down. All that matters is that you are all okay."

A nurse rushed in and gave him something to calm his nerves. "I am going to have to ask that everyone leaves and let him get some rest. He has been through a great ordeal and needs to relax a little bit."

Katie walked over, fighting back her tears, and kissed his forehead. "I will be back soon. I love you."

Jase didn't respond. He just doze off.

Katie and Rebecca went downstairs to the Pediatric floor to check on Michael once more. He was sitting up in the bed, playing with the toys that Rebecca had surprised him with.

"Michael?" Katie spoke up.

"Mommy!" He threw his arms around her neck. "Is daddy okay?"

"He is fine, sweetie. He is just resting. Would you want to go home with Aunt Rebecca tonight? She was going to take you and Athina."

"Okay, Mommy..." He was happy to go for a visit.

"Mommy will have to take care of daddy for a couple of days," Rebecca stated the facts. "But don't worry, I have ice cream in the freezer and we can watch some movies."

"Mmmm... I love ice cream." He chuckled.

Rebecca laughed. "I am going to get Uncle Derek ready and then I will bring your sister and you home."

"Okay, Aunt Becka."

While Rebecca was gone, Katie got Michael ready to go home. She packed up all of his toys and any clothes that had blood on them from the wreck. She felt sick in the pit of her stomach, imagining anything happening to the people she loved. She hugged Michael tight and kissed his cheek. "I love you so much."

He smiled. "I'm okay, Mommy. I love you too."

# Chapter 2

Jase had to stay in the hospital for a few days. When he woke up, he couldn't remember who Katie was or what had happened. His short-term memory was wiped clean, but he somehow remembered Michael.

"Who is she?" Jase asked the nurse as he pointed to Katie.

"Jase, that is your wife... Katie. Don't you remember your wife?" The nurse responded.

"I'm not married." He answered.

Katie's heart broke. "I don't understand. He remembered me when he woke up the other day."

"Sometimes, it takes a few days for head injuries to show serious signs." The nurse stated.

"Where is Michael?" He asked.

"He is at home with Rebecca," Katie answered.

"I'm sorry, you seem like a nice lady, but I don't remember you. Would you mind leaving?" Jase looked over at Katie with fear in his eyes.

"What?" She became upset.

The nurse pulled her to the side. "Give it a little while. He will remember eventually, it just might take some time."

"How much time do I give? What if he never remembers me? This is my husband." Katie had a tear fall from her eye.

The nurse rubbed her arm to comfort her. "I know it is hard, but you have to just have faith and believe that your love is strong enough to beat this."

Katie just nodded as she wiped the tear from her cheek. She walked over to Jase, who was still looking a bit confused as to who she was.

"Jase, I can bring you home if you would like?" She offered.

"No, I have no idea who you are. Please get my sister to get me." He refused to go anywhere with her.

"But, she is watching our children."

"I said get my sister."

He was so cold towards her. She didn't know if she could handle it much longer. This was not the Jase that she knew and loved. He was lost in his mind. A different person.

Katie left the room quickly and went into the bathroom to call Rebecca.

"Hey, Katie. Did you guys get home?" Rebecca asked.

Katie began crying hysterically. She could not pull herself together.

"Katie? What's wrong? Is Jase ok?" She worried.

"Yes, he wants nothing to do with me. He wants you to come to get him." She sobbed into the phone.

"Katie, calm down. I will be there shortly. It will be ok. I promise." Rebecca hung up and headed to the hospital while Derek stayed behind with the children.

Katie stood in the hospital room, waiting for Rebecca to show up. Jase continued staring at her with a puzzled look.

"Can I get you something?" Katie asked him.

"Look, I know that you are probably a sweet girl. And I am sure that we were probably happily married, but I don't remember that right now. I think until my mind comes back, maybe I should stay with my sister." He suggested.

Katie huffed under her breath. "Are you serious? That will keep you even further from remembering who I am. If you come on, something will trigger it to come back."
 "Katie, I just really feel that this is the best for me right now." He continued. "We can get together soon and try to rekindle our life together, but right now, I just need space.

"Fine..." She said. "Whatever you want. I will leave you alone."

She ran out of the room crying. Rebecca saw her and tried to get her attention, but she just kept running. When she got to the room, the nurse was unhooking all of the machines and helping him get ready to go home.

"Hey, sis." He smiled from ear to ear.

"Hey, Jase.  Are you about ready to go home?" She wondered.

"I told Katie that until I get my memories back, I would like to stay with you."

Her mouth almost hit the floor. This was not like him at all. "Jase? Are you sure that you should come home at all? I feel like more is going on because you are not acting the same."

The nurse began defending him. "He has a head injury. It is quite normal for him to behave this way."

Rebecca shot a look at the nurse. "No offense, but you know nothing about my brother. He may have short-term memory, but he always had a good heart. Now he is acting cold. I honestly don't believe this hospital knows what they are talking about."

The nurse rolled her eyes and pushed herself past Rebecca. Rebecca turned and look at her as she walked out of the room. "Bitch..." She muttered under her breath.

"Are you okay Rebecca?" Jase asked as he pulled his sneakers on.

"I am fine. I am just worried about you. Are you ok?" She asked.

"Never better. I am ready to go home and start this new life I have." He smiled as he walked past her.

Rebecca watched him leave the room, not understanding what was going on. This was not right. Something felt off. He had to have gotten hurt way worse than they thought.

Katie came home and everything was quiet. She was all alone. There was no laughing or crying. No Jase. She had no one that she could talk to. It was times like now, that she wished that she would have stayed in New York, but she wanted a new life and a new beginning. She just didn't think that this would be her new life.

Katie sat on the bed staring at a picture of Jase and her children. Just a couple of days ago, they were happy. Everything was normal. Jase had just spent the morning, making mad, passionate love to her, and then this happened and changed everything. She was not ready for this. She couldn't live here without Jase. She set the picture back on her nightstand and reached for her phone. She wanted to call, Sadie.

"Hello?" Sadie answered.

"Hey, Sadie." Katie tried not to let on she was upset, but Sadie could hear it.

"Honey, what's wrong?" She asked.

"Sadie, can you please come to visit with me. I am so broken." Katie sulked.

"Sure, I can be there in a couple of days. Are the kids ok?" Sadie worried.

"Yes, they are fine. It's Jase."

"Oh my God... What happened?" Sadie panicked. She was too far to get there right away.

"He is ok for the most part. He was in a wreck and now he doesn't remember who I am."

Sadie was quiet as she tried to take it all in. "You know, this is just temporary? He will be back to his normal self soon. Just try not to worry."
   "That's all I can do. I am so alone right now. He won't even come home with me, because he doesn't know me."

"I am so sorry. I will be there by the end of the week. I am sure he will snap out of it before then." Sadie comforted her friend over the phone.

"I know, I just feel so alone in this big house. My kids aren't home and now, Jase is gone. We were supposed to have some romantic time together this weekend."

"Things won't always be this way. It is just making the two of you stronger."

"Yeah, I know," Katie whispered under her breath.

"Try and get some sleep. It will be better soon." Sadie hung up after saying goodnight.

A knock came at the door. It was almost 8 at night. Katie grabbed her robe and walked downstairs. Maybe it was Jase. She opened the door to see a man holding flowers and a teddy bear. It had a card.

"Someone special had these delivered to you." The delivery man said.

Katie took the items and went inside. She sat the flowers and bear on the table and read the card.

*"My dearest Katie,*

*With every breath that I take, my love continues to grow. I could not ever think to love anyone, as much I love you. You make my heart long to be near you. The thought of touching you and feeling your skin against me brings so much joy to my life. I will forever cherish every day I have with you as my wife. I am looking forward to our weekend. I have big plans for you. I love you, Katie. In some ways, I loved you before I knew you. I can't imagine living this life with anyone else by my side. Keep smiling. It brightens up the room.*

*Love always,*
*Jase"*

He must have done this before the wreck. It brought a smile to her face, even though it was killing her on the inside to know that their weekend was over. Katie filled the vase with water and set the flowers inside of it. She then placed them on the fireplace mantel. She went upstairs and tried her best to get some sleep. It was not easy, but somehow she had managed to get some rest.

Jessica was still up to her old schemes with this mystery man. She knew this time she succeed in destroying the young happy couple. She was getting closer to finding them and set her plan in motion. She would make sure that her grandchildren would be kept safe and away from what she had planned for their mother and father.

This time, no one would know what hit them. Not even YOU...

"I have already started my plan. I know where they are and they have no idea what is about to hit them." The mystery man laughed.

"Good... I can't wait to see how this goes down." She admitted.

"When will I get paid?"

"In due time my dear... In due time." She walked over and fiddled with his shirt. "But I wouldn't mind rewarding you in other ways."

He grabbed her hands. He was firm. He lifted her in his arms and carried her to the room. She laughed all the way to the bed.

30 minutes later, the mystery man stood up and zipped his jeans. Jessica laid there admiring his hot physique. "My oh my, it has been a long time, since I had a young hottie like you in my bed." She ran her toes up to the crotch of his jeans.

He smacked her foot away. "Don't get too used to it. I am only going to fuck, when I want to," He spoke harshly. "Do I make myself clear?"

She just smiled as she bit her lip taking in the view of his chest. "I am willing to do other things."

"Are you so horny old cougar lady?"

"I can be for you. I am experienced."

"I have my eyes on someone else." He confessed.

"Who?" She sat up in the bed.

"Your daughter. I am going to make her fall in love with me."

Jessica leaped off the bed and grabbed him. "You listen here! You will not go after my daughter. She will never be loved again. She will be dead soon."

The mystery man grew cold-hearted and pushed Jessica against the wall and placed his hands around her neck. "Don't you ever get in my face again or the next time, I will make sure that you die." He dropped her on the floor.

Jessica coughed as she tried to regain her breath. She felt a little frightened that he would hurt her. She slowly lifted herself to her feet. The mystery man smirked at her as he straightened his collar. "Now, it was fun while it lasted, but I have to go."

"Where are you going?" She asked as she cleared her throat.

He turned and smiled. "That is for me to know and you to, well... not find out." He walked out of the room.

Jessica was worried. No one knew that she was alive and this guy seems to be out for revenge and doesn't mind taking her down with him. She knew she had to figure something else out and she had to do it soon. This guy was a loose cannon and had too much baggage.

A couple of days had passed, and Katie hadn't heard from Jase. Rebecca had brought, Michael and Athina home, since they were getting homesick. Katie looked miserable. It looked as though she hadn't slept. Sadie would arrive tonight, and Katie could not wait. She needed her friend, now more than ever.

"Katie, you should rest," Rebecca suggests as she put the baby in the crib.

Katie just sits on the bed and stares at the wall.

"Katie?" Rebecca sats beside her.

"I know you are going through hell right now, but I know my brother and this will not last long."

Katie began to sob into her pillow as Rebecca rubbed her back. "I miss him so much."

"I know sweetie. He just needs to get better and then he will be the man you fell in love with. He has fought off way harder things than this."

"What if he never remembers?"

"He will."

"But what if he doesn't. There is a possibility that he will never remember me or our love ever again."

Rebecca stood up in front of her. "Come here." She extended her arms out for a hug. "I need this as much as you do."

Katie stood up and hugged her. It felt good to know she cared and that someone would be there. She just wishes it was Jase.

"Go take a shower. I will watch the baby and Michael until you get out."

Katie went into the bathroom. Rebecca called Jase while she had a free moment.

"Hello?" Jase answered.

"Hey, Jase... I have to talk to you." She began.

"Ok, what's wrong sis? Is everything ok with my children?"

"Yes, of course. It's Katie that I am worried about."

"Listen, Rebecca, I really can't help that I do not remember her." He stated. "I want to, but I can't."

"But don't you want to try to remember?" She wondered.

"What kind of question is that? Of course, I do."

"Then maybe, you should come home and try to remember her instead of staying at my place, where you can't connect with her?" She validated her point.

There was a pause on the line for a moment. "Jase? Are you there?"

"Sis, I don't know how it will make a difference if I am there or here?" He replied.

"Seriously Jase?!" Rebecca was getting angry now. "This is stupid. She is your wife and the mother of your children. She has been through so much and you were never so heartless as you are right now."

She was right. He knew he wasn't thinking clearly. "I will come home tomorrow. I just need one more night."

"Fine, but just one more night and I am kicking you out." Rebecca joked. "I love you, but you have to go."

Jase giggled on the phone and then hung up.


# Chapter 3


Sadie had finally got there. She had her baby with her and a huge grin. Jackson had stayed home as he was busy taking care of the company. Montgomery Enterprises was growing and opened several branches around the country. Jackson was head of the California office now.

"I am so glad that you are here," Katie admitted. "I hate not being able to see you anytime I want."

"Me too. I have missed our afternoon lunches and movie nights we use to have." Sadie agreed.

Katie smiled even though her heart was broken.

"Hey, don't worry. He will come around. You just have to get through this storm first."

"It's just that I don't understand. He remembers our children, but not me. It doesn't make sense. Maybe he doesn't love me anymore."

Sadie rested her hand on Katie's lap. "Don't be silly. That man would move Heaven and Earth to be with you. He has been through hell for you, just so he could protect you."

"I know. Just something doesn't feel right." Katie couldn't shake this feeling she had.

"That's because Jase isn't here. Once he comes home, you will feel much better."

Anna, Sadie's daughter, began crying. "Let me get her. I will be right back." Sadie stated as she left the room.

Katie couldn't take it anymore. She wanted to hear Jase's voice, so she called him.

"Hello?" He answered.

It took her a second to speak when she heard his voice. "Hey, Jase. It's me, Katie."

"Oh, hi." He didn't know what to say.

Katie felt awkward. She knew she shouldn't have called. "I'm sorry, this was a bad idea." Her voice became shaky.

Jase could tell them she was having second thoughts. He began to feel bad for her. "Listen, Katie, I know that things are a mess right now, but it will get better. I am going to come home tomorrow and then I would like for us to work on getting my memory back."

"Really?"

"Yes, from what I have been told, you are the love of my life and I figure if you meant that much to me, then you are worth remembering."

"Ok, so we will take baby steps. I will do whatever it takes to get you back." She promised.

"I will see you tomorrow."

"See you then. I love..." She stopped herself. "Sorry, old habits."

"Don't apologize. This is not your fault. Talk to you later." He hung up.

She was glad she had called. She felt so much better, just knowing they were going to try and rekindle their love and break through this amnesia. She would not stop until he remembered who she was and the love they shared.

Sadie and Katie spent the day watching a movie and catching up on conversations they missed having. Michael had his friend from school over for a little while and the babies slept most of the day. It was nice having this time together.

Jessica was in town. She was keeping an eye on things the best she could since she didn't have the help that she thought she would have. She stopped by a hardware shop to buy some things she needed for her evil plan. She had bought some rope, duct tape, and a cloth bag. Her plan would still go on as scheduled and no one or nothing would get in her way. This time, she would succeed.

Jessica's phone rang and nearly gave her a heart attack. She quickly grabbed it.

"Yes?" She answered.

"Part of plan 1 is in motion." The mystery man spoke.

She was relieved and confused to hear his voice after he nearly choked her to death. "I didn't think that I would hear from you again."

"Are you still mad about that?" He chuckled. "That was foreplay."

She grew annoyed and wanted to hang up on him, but she had to see what was going on. "What are you doing?"

"I am watching her every move and learning her patterns." He began as he learked outside her window.

"She is sitting on the couch with her best friend. She looks delicious by the way. They both do."

Jessica snapped at him. "So now you have a thing for both of them."

He laughed. "I can't help what I crave. I can definitely see myself having a threesome with both of them."

"I don't have to listen to this anymore. Just do what you were paid to do, which is to destroy their marriage." She ordered him.

"Oh did I not make myself clear? I no longer work for you. I have bigger plans."

"You need me." She informed him.

He just laughed. "I don't need anyone. In fact, lose my number."
"If you don't cooperate, I will tell everyone who you are." She threatened.

"Go ahead, if you do that, you expose yourself as well."

She stayed quiet.

"What's the matter? Cat got your tongue?" He grinned. "Have a nice day and you stay out of trouble now." He hung up.

Jessica clenched her fist. She wanted to break something. He could ruin everything that she had planned. More importantly, he could expose her and let them know she was alive. She couldn't even think about that now. She had things to attend to at home that required her attention. She would have to deal with him later.

Katie had, later on, told Sadie, that she and Jase were going to try and bring his memory back by rekindling their love.  She knew that she could make him remember. Katie had gone upstairs to tend to Athina while Sadie stayed on the couch watching tv with Michael.

A shadow walked past the window. Sadie saw it out the side of her eye and slowly got up to see what it was. Michael was half asleep on the couch and her baby was in her bouncy seat. She crept over to the kitchen counter to see if she could see anything, but it was dark now and hard to see.

All of a sudden, she could see a man standing in a distance. She froze because the man looked like her deceased fiance, Michael. She couldn't even believe what she was seeing. "Michael?" She spoke under her breath.

"Aunt Sadie?" Michael walked in and scare Sadie.

She quickly looked back out the window and the man was gone. She was puzzled by what she thought that she had seen. "Yes, Michael honey. What's wrong?"

"I heard you say my name." He yawned.

Sadie lifted him in her arms. "I'm sorry. I thought I saw something, but it was just my mind playing tricks.

Sadie brought him to his room and laid him down on his bed.

"Aunt Sadie?" He asked. "Is daddy mad at my mommy?"

She kissed his forehead and tucked him in tightly. "No, honey. Daddy just has a booboo from the car accident and he and mommy are going to work on getting it fixed."

He yawned once more before falling asleep. When Sadie came out of the room, Katie was sitting on the couch. She could see that Sadie seemed pale. "Is everything ok?"

Sadie looked into the kitchen and then stared back at her friend. "Yes, I think I am just losing my mind." She laughed.

"You can talk to me."

"I thought I saw Michael outside. My Michael." She admitted.

Katie stood up. "Maybe you are thinking more about him since it is close to the anniversary of his death."

"Yeah, that could be it, but he has been gone for years now, so why would I hallucinate about him all of a sudden?" She was so confused.

"Sadie, it happens sometimes. It is a normal human response in coping with the loss of a loved one."

Sadie sighed. "Maybe you're right. It just felt real." She stated as she looked over at the kitchen window once more.

The next morning, Katie had to say goodbye to Sadie. She had to get back home to Jackson and she knew that Jase would soon be home to begin working on his memory.

"I will see you soon." Sadie hugged Katie.

"Not so long this time," Katie begged.

Rebecca had shown up to get the children so that Jase and Katie were left alone. She knew they would be a huge distraction and could interfere with them getting to spark up the memories. Jase walked in and things were awkward. It was like they were strangers.

"Listen, you two just take it slow. It will be ok." Rebecca promised.

"Thanks, sis. We appreciate you, keeping the kids." Jase hugged her.

Katie also hugged her.

"Anytime. I will bring them back next week."

Once Rebecca left, things were very quiet. Katie gave Jase a sympathetic, shy smile.

He walked over to her and took her hands in his. "Hey, you don't have to be scared around me." He tried to reassure her.

She felt stupid. This is her husband. Why does she feel like she is staring at a stranger? "I just don't know where to start."

He pulled her to him and planted a kiss on her lips. She quickly pulled away. "Whoa... We need to slow this down." She stated. "Baby steps."

He tried walking her up the stairs. "I think we should jump right in."

She pulled her hand away. "Jase? Slow down."

He seemed to get a  little annoyed that she wouldn't make love to him.

"I think we need to get your memory back before we make love."

He gave her a blank stare. "So, how do you propose that we do that?"

She honestly didn't know the answer. She just knew that she could not make love to him until he remembered her.  In her mind, it would be as though she was cheating on him.

"How about we look at some pictures and go from there?" She suggested.

He was a little disappointed. Like any other man, he wasn't thinking with the right head. He finally agreed to let her do things her way. He could tell that she was headstrong and would not have it any other way.

"Fine, we can try it your way first, but if that doesn't work, then I say we make love and see if that sparks a memory or two." He joked.

She smiled but shook her head no. "I will not make love to you until I know that you remember everything."

He rolled his eyes playfully but agreed. He wanted to see where this was going.

They sat on the edge of the bed looking through all of their pictures. With every picture, he had a blank stare. He didn't remember. He tried and he could tell her heart was saddened with each lost memory. He rested his hand on her knee. "Don't be sad. I will remember." He promised.

"I know baby. It is just hard knowing that you can remember everyone, but me." She admitted has her eyes began to swell.

He gazed at her and wiped a tear from her cheek. "My love for you is still there, we just have to work hard to get my memories back. I can still feel my love for you."

She felt hopeful, but it was still hard sitting next to him. It was too hard to connect with someone that didn't have the same feelings for her as she did for him.

He helped her to her feet and caressed her arm. "How about we order some food and maybe watch a movie?"

She agreed. Maybe that would help them both. It would give them a break from having to think so much about everything wrong.

Sadie had just made it home to Jackson, who met her at the airport. He had flowers for her and a huge smile. He was happy to see her and their daughter arrive safely.

Jackson walked over and threw his arms around her. "I missed you both so much." He kissed her.

Sadie laughed. "We were only gone for a day."

"That is too long." He helped her into the car and make sure Anna was safely bucked into her car seat.

As he walked around to put her luggage in the trunk an anonymous call came through on Sadie's phone. "Hello?"

There was a lot of static. She could barely hear the voice on the other line.

"I'm sorry, we have a bad connection." She informed them.

"Sadie?" The voice spoke again. "Stay away."

She couldn't tell who it was. It was very faint. "Who is this?"

"Don't come back." The voice demanded.

The phone disconnected. Jackson got in the car and looked at the confusion on her face. "Sadie? Are you okay?"

"Someone just called me, but I couldn't tell who it was or what they were saying, but it sounded as though they were warning me."

He was worried that someone was threatening his wife. "Do you have any ideas who it could be?"

She just shook her hand.

"If it happens again, I want you to let me know." Jackson made her promise.

"Of course. I will always let you know when something seems off." She promised.

"Don't worry though. It could have been the wrong number."
Sadie shook her head. "No, whoever it was, said my name."

Jackson felt a little uneasy. He didn't want his wife to be scared or worried. They had a great life together and he knew that she would constantly fear that someone was out to hurt her or their baby.

Back at Jessica's new hideout, she had a guest that was staying with her unwillingly. She had gone into the basement where she was holding them hostage. They were tied to a chair in the center of the room with a potato sack on their head covering their face and their legs were chained to the legs and their arms were cuffed behind their back.

She knelt down and whispered in their ear. "Don't worry, you will feel better once we get some food in you."

The person just wiggled in the chair, trying to break free. Jessica laughed as she walked away and closed the door behind her.

The person in the basement screamed out loud. They seemed to be in a lot of pain, but Jessica didn't care. She knew what she had to do next and would not let anyone get in her way.

Her phone rang. "Hello?"

It was the mystery man. "Do you have everything under control?"

"I thought you told me to lose your number?" She reminded him.

"I did, but I still have yours. I need you to keep our guests comfortable and well-nourished. They need their strength kept up, so they can help with the next part of my plan."

Jessica was angry. She didn't want to continue working with him. She didn't like taking orders from this guy.

"When will you let them know who you are and what you want because we both are out to hurt two different people." Jessica wondered.

He just grinned from ear to ear. "We are actually after the same person, you just don't realize that yet."

She was curious about that statement. "What are you talking about?"

"You will find out soon enough, but for now, just keep our guest in great shape." The mystery man ordered.

She felt like she had no choice like she was almost under his control. It was hard to tell him no.

"How come I can't tell you no? You seem to be in this for yourself.

"Don't worry about that right now. In time, you will begin to understand. Right now, you only have to know what I allow you to know."

The mystery man hung up.

Katie walked into the living room with a bowl of popcorn and notice that Jase was putting his phone down. "Jase? Who were you talking to?" She wondered.

"Oh, my sister. I was just checking on the kids and they were doing great. She said that Michael was getting ready for his bath and that the baby was fast asleep."

Katie smiled. "I wish I could have talked to Michael."

"I am sorry. I can call her back if you would like?"

She sat the popcorn on the coffee table. "No, don't be silly. I am sure they are fine and we have a date tonight."

During the movie, Jase draped his arm over her shoulder and scooted closer to her on the couch. She enjoyed feeling him next to her.

"There is a familiarness about this." He informed her.

She smiled. "We use to do this all the time before the baby was born."

"I think I remember that."

She was hopeful but was not happy that he was only thinking he remembered their moments together.

"Have we seen this movie?" He asked.

"Yes." She replied. "It is one of your favorite movies to watch with me."

"It is very good."

"We use to turn this off halfway and run upstairs to make love."

He looked at her, studying the expression on her face. "I can see why."

She blushed as she took a bite of popcorn.

He pushed a strand of hair behind her ear. "You have beautiful ears. You shouldn't hide them."

She began to get warm knowing that he was staring at her. "Maybe I should get us something cold to drink?" She stood up.

He tugged her back down on the couch. "Don't keep pushing me away. I promise I won't bite." He winked.

She felt uneasy. She didn't want to rush things with him. She wanted him to remember, but it was like he was a horny teenager.

"Jase, we have to take it slow. I want you to remember me." She admitted.

"Maybe this would be the fastest way to get my memories back?" He wondered.

She stopped to think for a moment. Maybe he was right? Maybe it would trigger him to remember? Maybe she should just give in and see what happens, but she wasn't sure she could. She wanted him to remember on his own. She needed him to remember their love.

Jase's phone rang. He looked down and saw who was calling. "It's the office. Can you give me a second to see what is going on?"

"Sure." She was relieved to see him walk outside.

Jessica ended up calling the mystery man once more. "I just fed our guest. They were not very happy about it." Jessica admitted.

"Please, call me Ethan. I feel like we keep talking in riddles with one another." The mystery man finally gave his name to her.

"Ethan? Why does that name sound familiar?" She wondered.

"Because you know me." He confessed.

"I don't know you."

"Yes, you do."

"How?" She was sure that she didn't know him.

"We work together." He admitted.

"You work for me?"

"Kind of. Listen, I can't go into details right now."

All of a sudden, someone approached Ethan. "Jase? Is everything ok with the office?" Katie walked up.

Ethan turned and smiled. "Yes, sweetie. Everything is just fine."

# Chapter 4

Sadie was home alone taking care of the baby while Jackson was at work. He had been staying late at the office since Jase had been out of it due to amnesia.

The baby was always crying and very colicky and barely slept. Sadie was exhausted. They hired a nanny to help give, Sadie, a break so that she would be able to take a nap and rest in between the baby screaming.

She had been hallucinating about Michael a lot. She saw him everywhere and heard his voice a lot. She even got to the point that when she would sleep, she would dream of him.

Her phone rang and nearly scared her half to death. She quickly answered it. "This is Sadie."

There was static on the other end of the line. "Sadie..." A voice cut in and out.

"Who is this?" She asked.

"You have to be careful." This time she heard the voice clearly. It was Michael.

"Michael?" Her eyes filled with tears.

"Listen, Sadie, you have to run. You're not safe. No one is." He warned.

She sat quietly trying to take it in.

"Sadie? Please run and never look back." He hung up.

"Michael? Are you there?" She cried when she heard the silence on the other end.

She had to be losing her mind. Michael is dead. She knew this. She didn't know how to respond to the warning. Why would he want her to run? Where would she even go?

The phone rang again and she answered immediately. "Michael?" She answered.

"No, Jackson." Jackson sounded worried on the other end. "Sadie, is everything ok?"

She pulled herself together. "Yes, I am just sleep-deprived."

"I just wanted to check on you. I am going to come home. I don't think you need to be alone right now."

"Jackson, I'm fine. It is just my mind playing tricks on me. I am just going to take a nap and I will feel better when I wake up."

"Are you sure?" He was hesitant.

"Positive. I will see you tonight." She hung up sitting the phone on the table.

Sadie got up and made sure that all of the doors were locked and set the alarm. The nanny was too busy cleaning the kitchen to realize that she was worried. She went into her room and laid down, trying to ignore the call from Michael.

Ethan was still busy trying to take over his twin brother's life. No one knew that he even had a brother, so it was working in his favor. He had already begun his plan and he was going to win Katie's heart and destroy everything that Jase loved more than anything in this world. There was more to this story than anyone had or could ever imagine. It didn't make sense yet, but Ethan would make sure that his story was told and that anyone that got in his way, would pay.

Katie was relieved to have her husband home, but she still felt uneasy around him. It was like a stranger was in her home. She loved him, but something didn't feel right. Michael and Athina were still at Rebecca's and Derek's place. They were coming home tomorrow. Katie spent time cleaning the nursery and Michael's room. She wanted them to have a nice comfy room to come home to.

All of a sudden, two big, strong arms wrapped themselves around her waist from behind. "Hey, there sexy." Ethan kissed her cheek.

She giggled. "Hi. What are you doing?"

"I remembered something." He informed her.

She smiled. She had waited so long for this moment. "What is that?"

He kissed her cheek once more. "I remember how much I love you."

Her heart fluttered. She turned to face him. "Are you serious?"

He just nodded.

"But how? I mean, I am glad, but surely you can't remember everything."

"It just all came back in flashes to me. I was watching TV and memories just flooded my mind."

She grabbed and hugged him tightly. "This is wonderful news."

"I agree." He lifted her in his arms and carried her out of the room.

"Where are you taking me?" She chuckled.

"I am making love to my wife. It has been long enough." He carried her to their bedroom and dropped her on the bed.

She watched as he pulled off his shirt exposing all of his rock-hard muscles. She never got tired of seeing him undress. It wasn't long before he was completely naked in front of her. She bit her lip with anticipation.

He crawled on top of her, kissing her neck and then moving his mouth to hers. He parted her lips with his tongue. He could feel her mouth tremble. "Are you nervous?" He whispered against her skin."

She grabbed him and pulled him firmer against her body. "I am never nervous when I am with you."

He sat up straddling her waist with his thighs and ripped her shirt open. Her breathing became faster as she grew more excited with every touch.

"You are beautiful." He cupped her round, soft breast in his hands.

Her body lifted in pleasure. "That feels nice"

He then stood in front of her and began to pull her pants off. "Wait..." She grabbed his hands.

He studied her facial expression. "What?"

"Tell me what you remember?" She begged.

He was now getting annoyed but didn't let her know. He had to play it cool or she would suspect something was wrong.

"How about we talk about that after we make love." He tugged at her pants once more.

She stopped him again. "Tell me about how we first met." She pressed for some answers.

"Um, we were at a party and your friend introduced us to each other and it was love at first sight." He made up something fast.

She frowned and sat up in the bed. She pulled her shirt together and walked past him to the bathroom.

He followed in behind her. "What's wrong?" He asked, pretending to care.

"We met at my mother's business. You had chosen me to design some clothes for your company." She began to cry.

He walked over to her and tried to comfort her the way his brother would. He wrapped his arms around her. "Don't cry. Maybe I am just confused.

"Jase, I can't keep doing this." She pulled away. "I love you and I will always love you, but I am not going to make love to a man that doesn't love me back."

"What are you saying?" He stared at her.

"I am saying that until I know for 100% that your memory is back, we will not make love. No kissing, touching, or cuddling, and from now on you can sleep on the couch."

"The couch? Really?" He now became aggravated.

"Yes, I can't share a bed with a stranger and that is who you are to me right now."

Ethan didn't even say anything. He just turned and walked away leaving her crying in the bathroom.

While Katie was upstairs Ethan made a call to Jessica once more. He was annoyed and wanted to make sure his plan continued as planned.

"Move on to the second part of our plan." He ordered Jessica.

"How do you suppose that I do that?" Jessica wondered.

"Figure it out."

"I am only one person."

"I don't care. I am ordering you to follow through with the second part of our plan or it is game over for you. Do I make myself clear?"

She could almost see the evil in his eyes. She knew not to cross him. "I will do what I can."

"You better succeed. There is no room for errors."

"Ok, I will do whatever you ask. What should I do with Jase?" Jessica wondered.

"Keep making sure he eats and stays nice and strong. We will need him to finish this once and for all." Ethan hung up.

Ethan turned around when he heard, Katie, walking down the stairs. She walked right past him and into the kitchen and began getting food out to cook.

Ethan walked in and sat at the table. "Listen, I am sorry that I lied to you. I just figured that if we made love, it would help."

She didn't say anything.

"Katie, Please don't shut me out." He grabbed her hand from across the counter.

She pulled her hand away. "We have been together for 6 years. This is the second time you have lied to me. The first time you lied was when you knew my mother and Dylan were back and we swore after that, that we would never keep secrets again, but you lied to get laid."

"It's not like that. I just really want to remember, so I will do whatever it takes to make that happen."

She just shook her head. "You are not the man I fell in love with."

He stood up beside the chair. "You're right. I'm not. That part of me is dead right now, but he is still in there. You just aren't willing to bring him back." He walked off.

Derek was busy getting Michael in bed. Athina was already sound asleep in her playpen.

Rebecca heard something at her door, but when she opened it, nothing was there. Derek walked out behind her scaring her half to death.

"You are a bit jumpy." He laughed.

"It's not funny. I heard something. It sounded like someone was outside our door." She worried.

He looked around but didn't see anything. "It was probably just the wind.

"You're probably right." She agreed.

Just then she noticed smoke coming from the kitchen. "Oh my God!" She grabbed Derek and ran to see what was going on.

There were no flames and it wasn't warm, but they couldn't see each other. "Derek? Where are you?"

"I am over here." He hollered.

Just then Rebecca felt a sharp object pierce through her neck. Her eyes grew heavy and she eventually passed out. Once the smoke cleared out of the kitchen,

Derek didn't see Rebecca anywhere. He ran to see if she was in the kids, but she was gone. He noticed that their kitchen door was opened so he ran out there to search for her, but she was gone. He hollered her name a few times, without a response. Someone took her.

He quickly called the police station. "Yes, my wife is missing."

"How long has she been gone?" The officer asked.

"This just happened. Our house filled with smoke and once it was clear, she was gone. Someone took her." He answered.

"Did you see who took her?" He was asked.

"What the hell didn't you understand?! I don't know. I couldn't see anything!"

"You need to calm down sir."

"Calm down! How am I supposed to calm down when my wife is gone?!"

"We are sending some officers to your home now. They should be there soon."

Derek quickly called Katie and Jase to let them know what had just happened. After hanging up they headed to their place to get the children and to see if they could help.

When they pulled up, the police were already there. Crime scene tape was set up all around the house.

Katie ran inside but an officer grabbed her. "You can't go in there."

"My kids are in there." She cried.

"They are fine," Derek spoke as he walked around the corner.

"Derek?" She ran to him and hugged him. " I am so sorry."

Ethan walked in right behind her. He had to pretend that he was just as upset as everyone else. "Does anyone know anything? How did this happen? Who is responsible? I will make them pay!" He rambled on.

Katie grabbed his hand to calm him down. "We need to stay calm for the children."

Dave, Jase's friend from New York showed up. He was now an investigator. Ethan looked at him with a confused stare.

"Hey man.." Dave walked over.

"Do we know each other?" Ethan wondered.

"Are you joking?" Dave asked.

Katie noticed that something was off. "You have to excuse him. He was in a wreck and has amnesia. Apparently, he forgot his wife and best friend."

Dave looked concerned. "I am sorry. I didn't know. I haven't heard from you in a while."

"Sorry, I have been preoccupied," Ethan spoke in an unpleasant tone.

"What brings you here?" Katie wondered.

"Well, I have been kind of watching over you guys in a way. There is something that you guys need to know." He started.

Katie and Ethan looked at him, with worry on their faces. "What is it?"

"That night that Jessica and Dylan died, we never found Jessica's body. She was gone by the time the paramedics arrived. I believe she is still alive and she is behind what happened here today." He tossed out an accusation.

"Wait? What?" Katie thought her life was going to get better, but her mother was still alive.

"And you didn't tell anyone?" Ethan grew furious. He knew he had to play it off and make it believable.

"I didn't want you guys to worry. That is why I have been watching over you guys." He informed them.

"You should have told us. We could have been watching out for each other." Katie cried,

"I have been watching out for all of you."

Ethan grabbed Dave and pushed him against the wall. "My sister is gone because of you!"

Katie was shocked to see how Jase was acting. She had never seen him get this way with the people he loved. This wreck has changed him a lot. "Jase? Let him go." She grabbed his hand.

Ethan did what she asked as Dave fixed his shirt. "I am sorry. I was only trying to protect you guys."

"Do you have any idea as to where, Jessica, would have taken my wife?" Derek spoke up.

"Not yet, but I do not believe she is any harm. I think she is trying to lure you guys to her." Dave answered.

"So you know everything?" Ethan wondered.

"Yes, I know everything?" David looked at him with disgust.

"Tell me then... Why is it that you had no idea that I was in a wreck?"

He paused for a moment and looked around the room. "Like I said. I was looking out for you guys. Once I knew for sure that Jessica was alive, I spent most of my time watching her."

Dave glanced over at Ethan. "That's not all. She is working with or for someone."

Katie dropped to the floor and began crying. "This will never end."

Ethan walked over and helped her up. "Stay calm. We will get her this time."

"You said that last time. She is always one step ahead of us. She never dies."

"Honey, calm down." Ethan hugged her. He did his best to comfort her the way that Jase would.

"Jase? Can I talk to you alone?" Dave wondered.

He was suspicious as to why he wanted to talk to him alone. What did he know?

"Sure." He kissed Katie's forehead and walked outside with Dave.

"What's going on?" Ethan asked.

"You tell me?" Dave handed Ethan some pictures.

Ethan took the pictures and looked over them. The pictures were of him and Jessica talking in an alley. "What is this?"

"Why were you meeting with Jessica?" Dave wondered.

Ethan had to come up with something quick. "Fine, you got me. I knew she was alive as well and I had paid her off to leave Katie and my children alone. I knew that she would keep coming back, so I did whatever I could to make sure she left us all alone."

Dave was still suspicious. "Why not tell your wife?"

"She had enough to deal with. I didn't want her to worry, especially since she had just had my baby."

"Hmmm. I see." Dave scratched his head and arched an eyebrow at him.

"You don't believe me?" Ethan grew anxious.

"I didn't say that. Just trying to figure it out." He walked off.

"Where are you going?" He asked.

"I am going back to my room to go over our leads. If anything else comes up, I want you to call me."

Dave left the scene. Ethan watched as he drove away. He would have to deal with that later. Right now he had to play the role of husband, father, and friend.

# Chapter 5

Dave was back in his room going over all of his leads. He put the pictures on a wall beside him and stared at them for a moment. "Something is going on. What don't you want me to know, Jase?"

He had known Jase for a long time, but something just didn't seem right. Maybe it was the wreck or the trauma they had all been through or maybe no one knew the real him. He pulled out a key that he found on the ground at Derek's. It may have been a clue or it could have belonged to Rebecca or Derek.

He called his buddies down at the police station and asked them to analyze it and see what they could find out.

Ethan and Katie had just gotten the children to sleep. It had been a long night. "How are you holding up?" Katie asked Ethan.

"It hasn't hit me yet. I guess in a way, I am just numb. Jessica keeps resurfacing and she is not going to stop medaling in our lives."

Katie rested her hand on his cheek. "We will put an end to her and all of her games."

He kissed the palm of her hand. "I know. I am just happy that I have you."

For a moment, she felt like her husband was back. "You will always have me."

He smiled at her. "How about you get some sleep? I have to check in with Derek and then I will join you."

She just smiled at him and slowly drifted off to sleep.

Ethan was well aware that he had to take care of Dave before he spills the beans on him. He was too close to discovering the truth. He wasn't going to let that happen.

Dave was asleep when he heard a noise inside his motel room. He grabbed his gun and slowly exited the room. He slowly walked out of the room looking from side to side, but he didn't see anything. "Is someone in here? Show your face!" He demanded.

No one came out and the noise had stopped. Maybe it was in his mind. He walked over to the table where his files were and they were untouched. He looked over everything and it was all in the same place. Just then someone put a bag over his face. He couldn't breathe. He grabbed at the person's hands, but they were far too strong. He kept kicking but it made it worse. Whoever this was, were way too strong for him. He gasped one last time before he passed out, and then finally his heart stopped beating. The killer dropped him on the floor. It was Ethan. "You just had to spoil my plans... Sorry, it had to end this way." Ethan smiled as he pulled the bag from Dave's face.

He searched Dave's body for any other clues and didn't find anything. He then took all of his files and boxed them up and carried them to his car, making sure no evidence was left behind. "Now to hide your body." Ethan lifted him in his arms and quietly carried him out to the car. Luckily no one was around to see him. It was a quiet night in Tennessee. Everyone had been asleep or too scared to come out at night.

Morning came around fast. Katie woke up to see Ethan staring at her with a smile. "Sleep well?" He asked.

She rubbed her eyes and yawned. "You're in a good mood." She noticed.

"I just feel like the luckiest man alive."

"How are you feeling today?" She wondered.

"Great, I am ready to start the day. Let's get my memories back." He leaped over her and began tickling her.

She laughed until he moved. She sat up on the bed. "Are you sure that you are ok? You seem rather calm for someone who just found out that their sister was kidnapped last night."

He sat on the edge of the bed. "I know we will find her and I know that she is ok."

"We don't know that. My mom is crazy and she doesn't care who she hurts to get what she wants."

"I just have a good feeling. I am going to make breakfast. Go wash up." He kissed her softly on her nose and left the room.

Katie was puzzled by how calm he was. It was like he didn't even care. This wreck made him a different person. She shrugged it off and ended up taking a shower before breakfast. When she finally came downstairs, Ethan was standing at the counter, talking to Michael who was playing with his toys.  Michael ran to Katie when he saw her and gave her a big hug.

"Mommy! I missed you!" He hollered.

She lifted him in her arms and gave him a big kiss on his cheek. "I missed you too.

Michael climbed down and leaped back into his chair and waited for breakfast to be served. Ethan was busy paying attention to what he was cooking.

The house began to stink of burned waffles. "Ewww daddy, it stinks!" Michael blurted out.

Katie laughed as she walked over and began helping Ethan with cooking. She continued giggling as she scraped the burnt waffle from the waffle iron.

Ethan looked at her and smiled. "Guess I am not one to cook."

Jase would always cook for them. He loved cooking fancy meals for his family. "I think we all mess up meals from time to time. Don't worry about it." She cleaned the mess and started a fresh batch.

Michael began to laugh. He found it to be quite amusing that his father had just burned breakfast.

Ethan looked over at Michael. He began to laugh himself and then slowly walked over to Michael. "Do you think this is funny?"

Michael nodded.

"Oh yeah?" Without another word, Ethan took some batter and smeared it across Michael's face."

He was in shock at first, but then grabbed a handful of batter and tossed it at Ethan.

The two of them ran around the house chasing one another. "Guys! You are making a huge mess and I just took my shower!"

"Awwww... Mommy never lets us have fun." Michael pouted.

Ethan grabbed him up into his arms. "She is right, Let's wash up before breakfast." He carried him to the bathroom.

When they returned, Katie had the entire table set. The guys sat down and began fixing their plates. "Yum." Michael licked his lips.

Katie watched this man who she believed was her husband. He had changed so much since the wreck that she barely recognized him. *"How could he be this calm? He is acting like nothing is going on. Doesn't he care about his sister?"* She thought to herself.

Jessica was busy keeping her guests well taken care of until Ethan gave her further instructions on what to do.

When she went into the basement, she pulled the sacks from their heads. Jase and Rebecca were both half out of it. Jessica walked over to Rebecca and tapped her shoulder. "Easy, you are ok for now," Jessica stated.

 Rebecca looked over and saw Jase sitting on the other side of the room. "Jase!" She hollered out.

 He was so weak, that he didn't move. He couldn't even muster up the strength to acknowledge that she was there.

 "You Bitch! What did you do to him?" Rebecca tried to break free, but she couldn't. She was way too groggy.

 "He is fine. He is just resting." Jessica lifted his face to make sure he was still breathing.

 "Let him go."

 "I can't do that. He is part of the plan as you are as well."

 "Just leave Katie alone. She has moved on. She doesn't even think about you anymore."

 Jessica walked over to her and smiled. "You silly little girl. This has nothing to do with me or Katie. This is about destroying his life."

 Rebecca was confused. "Why? He had nothing to do with you and Katie."

 "Do you not know anything? Someone wants to take over Jase's life."

 "But why would someone do that? The only one that could even pull that off is...." Rebecca turned pale white.

 "Ding... Ding... Ding..."Jessica grinned as Rebecca caught on. "Yes, Ethan is back."

 "But how?" She wondered. "He ran away when he was a child and we never heard anything from him since that day."

"I don't know the details, but I do know that he is out for revenge. He is not going to stop until he makes Jase pay."

"You can't do this!" Rebecca cried. "Jase didn't do anything!"

"I can't stop him. No one can." Jessica covered their faces once more. "I will be back soon with some food. Try to rest." She left.

Sadie was asleep on the couch while Anna was taking her nap. She began to dream of Michael and the love they shared. This dream was different. It was almost creepy and it was a warning, She was walking through a field and Michael was standing in the shadows of the flowers. It was dark and cold.

*"Michael? What are you doing here?" She asked.*

*"Sadie, you are in danger. I am trying to warn you, but you will not listen to me." He replied.*

*"I don't understand. How are you here?"*

*"I can't tell you right now. But I am warning you. Nothing is what it seems."*

*"What does that mean?"*

*"Open your eyes." He spoke in a more aggressive tone.*

*"Michael? Please just tell me." She cried.*

*"Open your eyes!" He hollered as she woke from her dream.*

Sadie was confused and frightened. What was going on? Was Michael warning her from the other side? Was she just imagining everything?

She looked over and saw that Anna was still asleep. She picked up the phone and called Katie. She felt like she had to check on her.

"Katie? Is everything ok?" Sadie panicked,

"Yes, we are fine. Someone kidnapped Rebecca last night. Dave said my mother is still alive. As of right now, we haven't heard from him." Katie confessed.

"Oh my God... How is Jase handling it?"

"He seems fine. Maybe a little too fine." Katie frowned.

"Katie?" Sadie sighed. "I have to tell you something."

Katie sat idol listening to her friend. "I keep seeing Michael. My fiance."

"Sadie, You know he is dead? You have to let him go now." Katie tried to let her down easily.

"This is different. He is warning us. He said we are in danger and that nothing is what it seems."

"What does that mean?" Katie wondered.

"I don't know. He told me to open my eyes." She tried to fight back her tears. "I feel he is warning us. Someone is going to hurt us."

Katie was quiet for a moment. "It wouldn't be that far-fetched to believe he could be warning us. Jessica is once again alive and well. Rebecca has been kidnapped and no one knows where she is. Maybe he knows her next move and he is trying to get you to keep your eyes open?"

Sadie began overthinking it. "What if Jackson is working with her this time?"

"What? No... Don't think that way. He would never hurt you like that. I see how that man looks at you." Katie tried to comfort her.

"Well, how far-fetched could it be? It seems like the people we trust most in this world are all in this thing together. They all want us to hurt and suffer."

"Jackson is not like that. Please don't do anything without talking to him first." Katie made her promise.

"I won't, but I can't trust him."

"I think you can. I don't think he is in on this."

Ethan walked in and overheard Katie on the phone. "Is everything ok?" He asked.

"Sadie, I have to go. Jase just walked in. Please just try and stay calm." She asked.

"Was Sadie ok? It sounded like you two were in some deep conversation." Ethan wondered.

"Yes, she has just been dreaming of Michael again," Katie answered him.

"And what is Michael doing in these dreams?"

All of a sudden, Katie felt like she couldn't trust Jase. There was something off with him. He didn't even seem upset about his sister being kidnapped. Maybe something was off with him and not Jackson.

"Nothing, you know how she gets sometimes. She starts missing him." Katie lied.

"Oh, I see. Maybe she should spend more time thinking about her husband and not her ex?" He was cold.

"Jase? That isn't fair. Michael isn't an ex. He was murdered and it was my fault."

"All I am saying is that she can't go on living in the past."

Katie stood up. "You have changed. Way too much. I understand that you have had a wreck and that it wiped your memory of me and your best friend, but it is as though you are another person. You are not the man I fell in love with."

"That isn't fair! I can't help it if I can't remember my life before this!" He leaped off the bed and pressed her against the wall.

She was scared to death. "Jase? What are you doing?"

"I want you to remind me. Remind me of the man I once was. Help me remember our love." Without another word, he planted a firm, passionate kiss on her lips.

Katie didn't feel it was right. She pushed him away. "Stop!"

"Come on, make love to me the way you use to." He became more aggressive with each kiss.

"Jase! I said NO!" She smacked at him.

He looked at her and saw the fear in her eyes. "I am so sorry. I don't know what came over me."

Katie had tears streaming down her face. She was trembling under his arms and he tried to comfort her. "Katie, please don't be scared."

"I think you should leave." She stated as she tried pulling herself together.

"Katie, I didn't mean to." He let her go.

"I need space. Just please leave." She asked once more.

"But?"

"I said LEAVE!" She pushed him away.

Ethan stared at her for a moment and finally left without turning back. She slid down her wall and sat on the floor and cried into her knees.

Ethan was furious. He stormed off, hopped in his car, and left. Katie had no clue as to where he was going or who he was running to. *"How could the man she loved, be so different? How could he treat her so badly? He was a new type of crazy that she just could not deal with."* She thought to herself.

Ethan went back to the place they kept, Jase and Rebecca hostage. He was pissed and he wanted to take his anger out on someone.

When he arrived he walked straight past Jessica and into the basement. He walked over to Jase and pulled the sack from his face and pulled his head back. "Wake up!" He demanded.

Jase began to open his eyes slowly. "What did you do to me?" He asked in a faint voice.

"My dear sweet brother, I have made you into the same monster like me." Ethan snarled at him.

"I feel different." Jase was still not understanding.

"Open your eyes and look at me."

"Leave him alone!" Rebecca demanded.

Ethan laughed as he walked over and injected Rebecca with a sedative. "Rest now little sis. I will deal with you later."
Ethan walked back over to Jase grabbing him by the hair again and pulling his neck back once more. "I said... Open.. your... eyes!"

Without hesitation, Jase did as he was demanded of him. Ethan smiled. "Good boy... The transformation has begun."

Ethan grabbed a mirror that was sitting on a table next to Jase. He held it in front of Jase. "Look!"

Jase looked in the mirror. He was horrified by what he saw. His eyes must be tricking him because his eyes were glowing red and he had dark veins under his eyes. "Am I dreaming?" He asked.

Ethan laughed. "If only it was that simple."

All of a sudden, Jase began having a sharp sensation in his mouth and he hollered out. "What did you do to me!?"

"You are now a blood-sucking monster just like me." Ethan finally confessed the truth.

Jase began to panic. "Let me out of here!" He demanded.

"Not yet. I have only just started. I still have to destroy your marriage."

Jase began to wiggle in the chair. "Don't you touch my family!"

He giggled in an evil tone. "But brother it is too late. The damage is already done."

He walked over to the door and turned once more. "By the way... Katie is amazing in the sack." He turned to leave Jase hollering at him.

"NOOOOOO!!!!!! You stay away from her!" Jase cried.


# Chapter 6


Sadie had gone to the grocery store while the nanny stayed back and watched the baby. She needed to get away and clear her mind. Everything she did lately, reminded her of Michael. She walked around the grocery store getting things she need for the house. She bought things the baby needed such as diapers, formula, and powder.

Once she left the store she got in her car and headed back home. All of a sudden she heard a familiar voice coming from the back.

"Don't be scared." The voice spoke softly.

She jumped as she looked in her review mirror.

"I will not hurt you." The voice explained.

She looked closer. She couldn't see his face, but something seemed so familiar. She knew this man that was sitting behind her.

"Who are you?" She asked.

"I think you know who I am. I have been trying to warn you now for days, but you have not listened."

"Michael?" She wondered out loud.

"Pull over down that alley."

She did ask what was asked. Once she pulled over and the car came to a stop, the man from the backseat climbed out and got into the front seat.

She slowly turned and looked at him. Her mouth dropped and her eyes teared. She slowly reached up and touched the man's face trying to see if he was real or only in her mind. "How?" She sobbed.

He took her hand and locked his fingers with hers and kissed her fingertips. "I have missed this." He admitted.

She cried as her heart ached. "Michael? I watched you die... I don't understand. Am I going crazy?"

He smiled as a tear fell from his eye. "Not at all."

"I don't know how this is real. I can feel you."

"I will explain everything to you. I am not the same man I was when we were together. I was turned into a monster. You are all in danger." He confessed.

She was confused. She was unsure of what that meant. "Monster? What does that even mean?"

"I would have to show you, but then you will be afraid and I can't let that happen. I can't live knowing that you are afraid of me."

"Michael, I need you to show me." She pleaded with him.

"Ok, brace yourself."

He looked away from her and when he looked back, his eyes were glowing red and the veins under his eyes were more pronounced. He had fangs and looked completely different. She gasped.

He quickly looked away when he saw the look on her face. "Look at me she said."

"No, I can't bear the thought of you being scared of me." He announced.

"Michael, look at me." She demanded once more.

He turned and looked at her. This time, he looked normal. His eyes were saddened and his bottom lip quivered. She rested her hand on his cheek. "I could never be scared of you." She admitted.

He began to cry on her hand and she grabbed him and pulled him in for a hug. "Who did this to you?"

"It was Jase." He blurted out.

Her heart stopped. He had to be wrong. Jase would never hurt anyone, but then again, this all started when he came into the picture. "Why would Jase do this?" She wondered.

"I am not sure, but it was him." He began to tell his story and what he remembered. "I was dead. Cold in the morgue and I woke up to a piercing sharp pain in my neck. I remember looking to the side and Jase was standing there with blood dripping from his fangs. I remember feeling my lungs fill with air and my stomach was so empty feeling. It was the worst type of hunger pain a person could ever imagine. All of my memories of my life from the time I was born until I died filled my mind. I could remember things, that people should not remember. I remember being born. I remember being in my mother's wound."

Sadie was in shock. She didn't understand how any of this could be real. "Why didn't you come to me sooner?"

"And do what? Scare you? Scar you for life? I knew if you had seen me back then, you were too weak to handle it, but you are stronger now and that is why I came back."

"But Michael, I loved you. I love you..." She blurted out. "And now I am married to Jackson and he is a great man, but he's not you." She cried.

He stared at her for a moment with sympathy in his eyes and pain in his heart. He was in love with her, even after everything he had been through. He was so angry that Jase destroyed their lives. "Sadie, you have to move on. I can't give you what you need anymore."

"Yes, you can." She grabbed him and kissed him.

Michael didn't stop it. He had longed for her lips to be on his for years. He missed the taste of her kiss and the feeling of her warm skin against his. He needed this as much as she did. He ran his hands through her long, silky hair and pulled her head closer to his mouth. "You have no idea, how much I have missed you."

"Yes, I do because I have missed you as well." She admitted as she kissed him once more.

Sadie's phone rang and brought them both back to reality. It was Jackson.

Michael saw his name on the phone and stayed quiet as she answered it once she caught her breath. "Hi, Jackson."

"Hey, is everything ok? I called the house first and the nanny said that you had been gone a while." He worried.

"I'm sorry. I had to run some errands. I am on my way home now." She informed him.

"It's ok, I just worry about you. I would die if anything ever happened to you."

Her heart broke a little more hearing him say that. Michael could hear the whole conversation. He knew that he had to let her go. It wasn't fair that he came between them.

"I will be home soon. I will see you tonight." She promised.

"I love you, Sadie," Jackson spoke softly.

She frowned because she knew Michael was there. "Me too." She replied.

At that moment, Jackson knew something was different. She would never hang up a phone call from him without saying "I love you too."

Michael turned and faced her. They both had tears in their eyes and he took her hand in his for the last time. "Go be with your husband. He is alive and can take care of you. I only came back to warn you all. Jase is not who he seems."

"But I don't want him. I want you. I was supposed to marry you." She grabbed him, but he pushed her away.

"Damn it, Sadie! I should have never come back. I have to go. Run and never come back." Michael got out of the car.

Sadie got out behind him, but he was already gone. She leaned against her car and cried. She couldn't live without seeing him anymore. The pain was too much. She knew that she would have to get home and take care of her daughter and be a pretend wife, because she knew in her heart, that Michael was all that she wanted. She loved Jackson, but not like she did Michael. The void was always there. She knew that she would have to find Michael and this time, she would not stop until she had.

When she arrived home, she made sure to fix her make-up and hair and tried to pull herself together. She knew that she had to pretend as though nothing was wrong. She had to be strong for her daughter. She walked inside where the Nanny was holding the baby and tried to get her to stop crying.

"Brandi? How long has the baby been crying?" Sadie wondered.

"She just woke up. I think she missed her mother."
Brandi the Nanny handed the baby over to Sadie.

Sadie grabbed a bottle and began to feed Anna. She
quiets down instantly. "She was just hungry."

"Yes ma'am. I am sorry. I tried to feed her, but she
wouldn't take her bottle for me."

"It's ok. I have it from here. You may go home." Sadie
encouraged her.

It wasn't long after the Nanny left that Jackson got
home. He walked in holding some flowers and a cake.

"What's the special occasion?" Sadie asked as she laid
the baby in her bassinet.

He walked over and handed her the flowers. "No
occasion. I just want you to know that I love you."

She just smiled.

"Sadie? Is everything ok?" He worried. "I mean with
us?"

"Of course. Why wouldn't they be?" She turned to put
the flowers in some water in a vase.

"Twice today, I have told you that I love you and you
won't say it back. That isn't like you. Did something
happen?"

"I'm just tired." She lied.

"I don't believe you." He admitted. "You keep talking
about how you keep seeing or hearing Michael's voice
and now all of a sudden things feel different with us. I
feel like you are drifting away from me."

She turned to face him. "Jackson, we are fine. I just
went through some relapses with Michael, but now I
am over it. We are fine and I love you. I am sorry that I
made you question how I feel for you." She walked over
and kissed him. "Thank you for the flowers. They are
beautiful."

He reciprocated the kiss and held her tightly in his arms. "You are my lady and I can't compete with a ghost. I just want to know that you can talk to me about anything."

"I know and I will. I am fine though. How about we go to our room and I will show you just how much I love you." She began walking him to the bedroom.

Jackson followed her into the room. Anna was sound asleep. She began unbuttoning, Jackon's dress shirt and slowly tossed it on the floor. He walked her over to the bed and lightly pushed her over the bed onto her back. He leaned down and planted a kiss on her lips.

He then ripped her shirt off and threw it on the side of the bed, making her moan. He yanked her pants off and let them drop to the floor in front of him and then dropped to his knees and parted her thighs with his hands and let his mouth meet her warm, moist center. She was inviting as she felt his tongue dip inside. She cried out, reaching for his hair. She helped guide his mouth the way that she wanted to feel it move around.

He then stood up and pushed himself inside of her, making her body arch with pleasure. She was tingling all over. She wanted this. She loved the way he felt inside of her. He filled every inch of her tight, juicy, spot.

He pushed harder and faster. He was firm but gentle, He was like a beast in the bed. She cried out asking him for more. "I need you!"

The sound of her plea turned him on even more. He lost all control. He leaned in taking her nipple in his mouth and gave it a gentle tung with his teeth. She loved it.  He then moved his mouth to her neck and began kissing and sucking, leaving his mark on her. "You're mine. " He whispered in her ear.

At that moment, she knew he was right. She was his at that moment. She loved Jackson, but she also loved Michael.

She had to stop thinking of Michael while she was making love to Jackson. She had to distract her mind from what she truly wanted. She couldn't hurt Jackson that way.

Jackson pounded her even harder until he finally let go and exploded all of his white, creamy, pleasure inside of her. "You are amazing." He dropped onto the bed beside her.

She rolled over and smiled as she played with the curly, dark hairs around his nipples. "Jackson, I really do love you.

"I know you do, baby." He leaned over and kissed her nose. "I am going to take a shower. Feel free to join me."

Jackson stood up and walked to the bathroom.

"I will be right in." She promised.

Sadie looked at her phone to make sure that Michael hasn't called her. She had no missed calls. She felt disappointed and knew that she had to stop thinking of him. He made it quite clear that it was over between them, but he also made it clear, that they were in danger.

She had to warn Katie about Jase being behind everything, but she had to have proof. Katie could never believe that Jase would be so horrible. She couldn't even believe it herself, but then Katie said to herself that Jase had been different.

She grabbed her phone and began to dial Katie's number.

"Sadie? Are you going to join me?" Jackson interrupted her.

She sat her phone down and headed into the bathroom to join her husband. She didn't want him to know right now. He would not believe her, but she knew and hoped that Katie would listen to her once she confessed that her dead fiance was very much alive and was a vampire.

# Chapter 7

Ethan had been staying with Derek since Katie kicked him. He wanted to make her resent him and had no intentions of making things right between them.

Ethan rummaged around the house, looking for anything he could, later use in his plan to hurt Jase. He found pictures of him, Jase, and Rebecca when they were children. He then stopped when he came across one of their parents. His eyes swelled as he remembered the pain that his siblings were so easily able to forget. It was what made him who he was today. He threw the box of pictures across the room in a rage.

Derek walked in a saw the pictures scattered around the room. "Are you ok?" He wondered as he knelt down to pick the pictures up.

"Yes, sorry. I am just so angry that someone has my sister." He lied.

"Me too. I can't believe no one has found her yet and all I keep thinking about is what if it is too late?" Derek sighed.

"Don't think that way. If I know anything, I know Rebecca is one strong, bad-ass woman and she will get away."

"I know she will, but I hate the thought of her being held, hostage.  She has to be so scared and I am not there to comfort her. She needs me."

Ethan walked over and rested a hand on his shoulder. "I know. We will find her. Just don't let this get in your head. I am sure that she is closer than we think."

Ethan knew exactly where she was. She was not far at all. He had to keep pretending to be Jase and making everyone love him until he could get them all where he wanted them. He didn't want anyone to suspect a thing.

Derek stood up. "Have you heard from Dave?" He wondered.

Ethan almost forgot about his so-called friend. "No, I haven't. I am sure he will contact us as soon as he knows something."

"I just assumed that by now, he would have at least contacted us to let us know if he knew anything at all."

"Maybe he doesn't want to give us false hope?"

"I just wish there was a way to find the. Jessica needs to be killed. I hate to say that, but the next time I see her, I will personally kill her myself and I will make sure she is dead." Derek threatened.

"I will help you." Ethan offered. "I will drive a knife through her cold, black, heart."

Derek looked at Ethan, shocked to hear him talk that way. "You seem different, Jase."

Ethan noticed the side-eye stare that he was getting. "I have changed. With everything that lady has put us through, how could I not? I want to rip her head from her body and watch as her bloodless body falls to the ground."

Derek stood up. "Listen, I have to go down to the station. I want to see if they have any leads. Tomorrow, I plan to search for her myself. I can't just keep sitting here."

Ethan agreed. "I will go with you. I have nothing to go back to now that Katie kicked me out."

"Why don't you call her and work things out? She is in a vulnerable place right now." Derek encouraged as he walked away.

Katie was sitting at the table in the kitchen when her phone rang. It was Jase. She ignored his call. She couldn't deal with him right now. Not after last night. She turned the ringer off on her phone and tended to Athina, who had been crying.

Her son, Michael was at school and she had things that she had to get done before she had to pick him up. She knew that she was only trying to fill the void for Jase by keeping herself too busy to think about it.

Sadie had tried calling Katie several times but kept going right to her voicemail. "Katie, please call me as soon as you get this message." She left a voicemail.

Jackson came downstairs after getting ready for work. "Sadie, I have to go. I will see you tonight?"

She walked over and kissed him goodbye. "I love you."

"I love you too, Angel." He reciprocated the kiss.

Once Jackson left, she began packing her stuff. She had called the Nanny and asked her to stay with the baby for a few days. She had to go be with Katie and make sure that Jase didn't hurt her. She knew that she should tell Jackson, but she couldn't take the chance of him getting hurt or worse, running into Michael. She couldn't even tell him that vampires really do exist and that they are after all of them. She had never been so scared in her life. It was bad enough when Jessica was after them, but throw vampires into the equation and that is a nightmare worth waking up from.

She grabbed her bag and headed to the airport on the next flight to Tennessee.

Jessica stood in the basement watching Jase and Rebecca. They both had kept falling in and out of consciousness and seemed to be rather weak.

Jase began to wake up. "Please... let my sister go." He begged.

Jessica didn't respond.

"Jessica? I know that you are there... I can smell your flesh and I can hear you breathing from across the room."

She walked over to him and pulled the sack off of his face. He was sweating and gasping for air. It must have been really hot under that sack. She held a cup of water to his parched lips. "Drink."

He took a sip of the water, quenching his thirst. He looked up at her. She didn't seem to be the same monster that he had loathed. She seemed to sympathize with him. "You can't keep doing this. Eventually, they will catch you."

She sighed. "Listen, I don't know why I do half the things I do these days. None of this makes sense." She began. "It was like one day, I just woke up and I felt this rage for my daughter and I didn't want her to be happy. I honestly cannot explain it."

"Maybe someone else is making you do this?" He wondered.

"How could someone make someone else do something? What kind of mother tries to kill their daughter?"

"You can fix this. Let Rebecca and I go. You don't have to keep repeating the same patterns."

"I can't." She sighed.

"Jessica? Look at me..." He asked of her.

She slowly lifted her gaze. "I can't go against him. He will kill us all."

"I can protect you. I am a monster just like him. I have the same abilities as him."

"Why would you help me? I kidnapped your children and tried to kill you both. I even killed your friend. I have destroyed so many lives." She felt different all of a sudden. The hate she had felt for her daughter was gone.

"Jessica, I think you are under some type of hypnosis or something. I don't think you did this on your own. You are confused."

She snapped herself out of a weak moment. "No, I see what you are doing? You are distracting my mind with these assumptions, hoping I will have a better heart and release you guys, but you are dead wrong." She grew angry.

She grabbed Jase by the face and got real close. "I hope you and Katie both die and I hope I get to watch as you drink the blood from her veins and leave her lifeless on the ground as I spit in her face. Then I hope the pain becomes too much and you take your own life because that is what the both of you deserve. " She laughed.

Rebecca woke up and hollered out. "Leave him alone!"

Jessica pulled the sack from her face and smacked her across the face. "You shut the hell up! I will kill you right now if you make one more peep."

Jase and Rebecca kept their mouths shut. They didn't want to anger her any more than they had.

Her phone rang. It was Ethan. "Hello?"
"How are they holding up?" Ethan asked.

"They are fine. They seem to have more strength today. They are a bit feisty." She replied to him.

"Good, before long, they will both be ready."

"Ready for what? Are you going to fill me in on what you have planned for them?"

"You will find out everything soon. It will all begin to make sense to everyone." He laughed as he put his phone in his pocket.

Jessica was so confused and worried about what he was up to. She knew that they were no longer on the same team and she was scared. She wanted to run away and hide, but she knew that he would always find her and that when he did, he would kill her or worse. He might even torture her as he has with Jase and Rebecca.

He had too much dirt on her and she knew that if she betrayed him, all gloves were off. She had to play it cool and not let on that she was done playing by his rules. She was not going to help him. She was out for herself and at that moment, no one else mattered to her.

Sadie's plane had just landed. She grabbed her luggage and grabbed the first cab that would stop. She climbed in after placing her suitcase in the trunk.

"Please take me to 96 west oak st." She instructed the driver.

The driver nodded in approval and drove away.

Derek was at the station and began talking to the other officers. No one had heard from Dave, since the night Rebecca was kidnapped. They had gone to his motel and discovered that someone had been there and had taken all of the files.

"How the hell can Jessica keep getting away with all of this?" Derek went mad. He slammed his fist on the desk.

"Derek? My name is Officer. Lampkin. I understand that this is hard, but you have to calm down. Something will turn up and when we find Jessica, we will find your wife."

Derek didn't believe him. "At this point, she could already be dead."

"You have to have faith. I don't feel she is in danger. I believe she is more of a bait."

"That doesn't make this situation any less fucked up."

"I agree. And we are doing everything in our power to find her. We have some footage of the person who broke into the motel room the night Dave went missing. We are having to have it analyzed as the vision is very blurred on the tape. Forensic is backed up right now, so that could take a couple of days to get. In the meantime, I think it would be best for you to go home."

"And do what?" Derek snapped.

"Sir, if she comes home, I am sure you would be the first face she would like to see."

"Yeah... If she comes home." Derek gave him a dirty look and walked away.

Sadie noticed that the cab driver was going the wrong way. She began to feel uneasy about the drive there. "Excuse me, I think you went the wrong way?"

He turned to face her. "You didn't listen to my warning," Michael said from the front seat. "I told you to run away."

"Michael? What are you doing here? How did you find me here?" She asked.

"I know everything. I watch every move you make because I know that you need my protection."

"I am ok Michael. You don't have to watch over me. Katie is who needs protecting." She blurted out.

"You don't think I know that? I am watching over her as well. I would never let anything happen to your best friend. I know that would kill you, but right now..." He paused.

"What Michael?" She scooted closer to the back of his seat. "What were you going to say?"

"I can't let anything happen to you Sadie. I still love you. I never stopped." He sighed under his breath. "Even after all of this time and all of these years, you are and will always be the only woman for me."

Her eyes became full of tears. She tried to blink them back but she couldn't. So many lives were at stake and she knew that she would have to make a decision. She loved both Michael and Jackson, but her heart would always belong to Michael a little more. If he hadn't died, she would have been his wife. She could never let that go, but now she and Jackson have a daughter together. Things were very complicated and she didn't know what to do. Either way, someone was going to lose and have their heartbroken.

"Your turn. Say something." He pulled over.

"Damn it, Michael!" What am I supposed to say? You died... I watched you die..." She scooted closer to the back of the seat. "I moved on Michael. I have a family now.."

He got out of the car and opened her door and help her out.

"Tell me you don't want me. Tell me that you haven't spent every day of the last 6 years thinking about me." He pressed her body against the car.

"Don't..."

"Then tell me that you don't love me."

"I can't do that." She cried again.

"Why not?" He pressed for an answer. "Why can't you say it, Sadie?"

"Because I never stopped loving you!" She finally screamed out.

Without another word, Michael pressed his lips to hers and made love to her mouth with his tongue. "I have missed this. I needed to feel your touch, your lips, your skin. I have ached to be inside you. I want you to make love to me."

For a moment she thought about it and then pushed him away. "Michael, I can't. Not while I am still married."

"Are you going to leave him?"

"I think it is only fair if I do. I can't lead him on and keep making him think that there is hope for us. He has to know that my heart is still yours."

Michael smiled as he stared deeply into her eyes. "And you're ok being with me knowing that I am now a vampire?"

"Of course I am. Nothing can change the way I feel about you." She kissed him once more.

He liked the sound of that. "Good because this time I promise I am not going anywhere."

She was excited to see where this new life would lead. She knew that Jackson would understand and that he would be hurt at first, but then realize that it was for the best. "Where are we going?"

"I am taking you to my hideout. You will be safe there until I get back." He filled her in.

"Are you not staying?" She grew fearful of being on her own in a strange place.

"Sweetheart, I have to go watch over Katie. She doesn't know who she is dealing with and she is in more danger than anyone."

"Enlighten me... Just how much danger is she in?" She was disquieted.

"I think he plans on turning her. I am not sure right now, but he is going to make Rebecca and Dylan look like saints."

Michael rushed her back to the hideout. It was a nice little house in the woods. Nothing was around for miles. Not even a grocery store. She looked around feeling bothered by the idea of being so alone and secluded from the rest of the world. She wouldn't even have a phone because it could be traced.

He could see the distant look in her eyes and the doubted concerns that she must have. He wanted her to feel at ease, but he knew that she couldn't. She was horrified and why wouldn't she be. She was going to be by herself in the woods.

Michael lifted her chin and gazed into her eyes. "Look at me, Sadie. I would never put you in any type of danger. You can trust me."

"But I will be alone?"

"For now. I will be back before you know it and then you and I can start our future together."

A bunch of thoughts began to weigh heavy on her mind. "How do you walk in the sunlight if you are a vampire?"

"Everything you watch or read about Vampires is a myth. Yes, we drink blood and we have eternal life but we can eat garlic, we can control our urges, and we are even better in bed. "He winked. " We have a strong sex appeal that has women throw themselves at us, however, I only have eyes for you."

She began to feel a little better knowing this stuff. "Can you be killed?"

He nodded. "Yes, but only by decapitation. If we are injured in any way we heal."

"Are you going to turn me?" She took his hand and studied his face.

"I would never turn you unless you ask me to." He assured her.

"How do you turn someone?"

Her questions were piling on and he didn't know how much more he would have to answer. He knew that she was stalling him out of fear. "I would have to bite you.

Not just any bite. I would have to suck the blood from your neck until you are near death. Once you heal from that bite, I would have to bite you a second time to complete it, and then you would have to feed to complete the transition."

"Does it hurt?"

"Sadie? I really have to go. I know what you are doing, but if I do not leave now, it may be too late to save Katie. I promise that you will be just fine here. There is plenty of food and I even have cable. In the room, I have some books by your favorite Author Lisamarie Hunter." He smiled.

"You remembered." She hugged him as though she would never see him.

"I remember everything." He admitted.

She wanted him to open up to her and reminisce about their love. He moved towards her and pulled her into his arms. "I remember the way that we would dance in the kitchen while dinner was cooking and the way you would stare at me while I was in the shower and you thought I hadn't noticed. Your quirky little habits would drive me nuts, but excite me at the same time, like biting your nails when you were scared. I remember the smell of your lavender bubble bath. It would fumigate the entire house. I also remember that every time we made love, it was like we were making love for the first time all over again. Not a day went by that our love didn't intrigue me. I was completely and utterly mesmerized by you."

She pulled her hands away. Her heart fluttered. She was fixated on the words "was". "Have you stopped being mesmerized by me?"

"Listen, we have a lot to work through, but I really have to go. When I get back we will talk about everything and figure this out." He leaned in to kiss her forehead, but she stopped him.

"Let's just wait until we talk. I will be here when you get back." She promised.

He walked away without another word. Sadie had walked around the cabin. Everything was well decorated and there were pictures of her and Michael on the mantel. The fridge was fully stocked with almost everything she loved.

She decided that she would take a shower and try to wash some of the adulterous thoughts from her mind. How could she be in love with two men and most importantly, how could she hurt one of them?

She turned the water on in the shower and waited for it to heat up. She put the radio on and listened to the voice of the singer and the words in his voice that sent memories flooding back once more of her and Michael.

*"Maybe he didn't love her anymore? Maybe she was just a distraction for him now? Maybe he has moved on as she had? Maybe it had been too many years."*

She saw a shadow standing outside the shower. It was Michael. He was completely naked and he opened the door to the shower. He stood there looking at her with a hunger in his eyes. He wanted her and he wanted her now.

"Michael? What are you doing?" She pretended to care.

"Fuck it." He growled under his breath.

He spun her around and pressed her wet, silky body against the wall. Her back was pressed against his chest and her breasts were firm against the wall. She turned one cheek to look at him and he leaned in and kissed her soft at first on the nape of her neck. Her legs buckled on her and he held her tighter so that she would not fall.

"I have wanted this for a long time. I have missed this." She cried out.

"Don't talk. Just let me fuck you the way a vampire fucks!" He yanked her hair and tilted her head back.

He pulled her off the wall still having her face in the opposite direction as grabbed her breasts and gave them a firm squeeze. It was painful but pleasurable. She was enjoying it. She wanted more.

He felt stronger than he had ever been and more confident. He was never this wild in bed. Maybe he had been craving this for far too long? Maybe being gone for so long has changed his desires? Sadie didn't care. She just wanted him and she would settle for whatever he had to offer.

He spun her around to face him and he demanded her to get on her knees in front of him. He firmly pushed her down. "Put my cock in your mouth!" He grabbed her by the head and pressed his manhood into her warm, hungry mouth.

The feeling of his fucking her mouth was intense and erotic. She was enjoying him being controlling of everything. She wanted him to possess every inch of her. He continued to penetrate his erection in and out of her mouth while guiding her head back and forth. The way her tongue felt against his dick excited him. He then yanked her up and once more pressed her chest firmly against the wall as he bent her over. He smacked her firm-round ass and grabbed her long, brown, wet hair, and then quickly nudged himself inside of her.

It was like an explosion of feelings went off in her mind and her body needed more. She had never been ravished this way before. It was so damn hot and she couldn't get enough.

"Please don't stop." She begged as her cheek was planted against the wall of the shower.

"I said... Don't speak!" He smacked her bottom one more time.

He thrust his cock in and out of her repeatedly in long, hard strokes. Her knees began to shake. "Spread your legs." He lifted her a little higher.

She couldn't take it anymore. She released her milky, white cream all over his shaft. He let her body fall limp.

"I'm not done!" He lifted her into his arms and carried her into the room.

Michael slammed her warm, naked body down on the bed and pressed himself inside of her achy, moist inviting core. He fucked her real good. She didn't think she could take much more.  She was sore, but she wanted him to continue until he finished. When he felt she had enough, he gave one final hard thrust and came inside of her, leaving her breathless and very tired but very well appreciative.

He plopped down beside her feeling out of breath. "Don't you ever think that I stopped loving you?"

She sent a smile in his direction. "That was amazing."

He pulled her towards him and held her in a strong embrace. He kissed the top of her head and just laid there quietly for a moment.

"What are you thinking?" She wondered.

"That I need to go rescue your friend, because if I don't leave soon, Jase will get to her before I have a chance and she has two kids there that need her."

She stood up and winked at him with approval. "Please go. I will be here when you get back. I promise."

He leaped out of the bed and gave her a kiss that told her that there would be plenty more nights like this to come.

Chapter 8

Katie stood staring into the darkness of her window. She missed Jase and didn't like this new version of him. He seemed unrecognizable lately and it was as though he only wanted the sexual parts of her and not the actual love parts.  She felt miserable and lonely without him being there. She wanted to get away and clear her mind, but she had her children to think about. They need her to be strong. It wasn't easy to smile around them knowing that their father was a different man now.

A knock sounded at her front door. Katie was startled as she was not expecting anyone and it was the middle of the night and she was home alone with her two children. She grabbed a knife from the drawer. She slowly approached the door. "Who is it?" She called out.

It was quiet for a second, but then she finally heard a familiar voice on the other side of the door. "It's me... Jase."

She let out a long exhale when she heard his voice. She opened the door and stared at him not inviting him in. "What are you doing here?" She spoke with an attitude.

"We need to talk. May I come in?" He cocked a sympathetic stare her way.

"We have nothing to talk about."

"Seriously Katie? You are my wife and mother of my children. I think we have plenty to talk about."

After pondering the thought for a moment, she let him come inside.

"Are the kids in bed?" He looked around.

"Yes. It is the middle of the night."

He was getting frustrated with her quirky attitude. "Will you knock it off already? I get it. I fucked up, but only because my head is scrambled up from the amnesia."

She sat on the couch with her knees pulled up to her chest. "I understand that Jase, but everything is different."

He sat down beside her and stared at her intensely. "I have no intention of getting you in the sack anymore. I really want to make this work and trigger my memories. I know that I love you."

She frowned. "How can you know that, if you can't even remember me?"

"It's just a feeling that I have." He ran his hand up her leg to comfort her. "Katie? I didn't choose this. I would never choose to forget the one thing that was good in my life."

"I know and that is why it makes this even harder. I want to make love to you, but I can't. You're not my husband."

Ethan looked over at her. Had she finally figured the truth out about him? "Are you wanting to get a divorce?"

She was reluctant to answer, but she already knew what she wanted and Jase was her everything. She could never divorce him. They had too much history together. "No... Of course not."

He was oblivious to what was going on. He needed her to explain what she meant because if she somehow figured out his plans, he would have to kill her sooner than he had planned.

"I am saying that maybe we should try to make love? Maybe you were right and this will trigger all of your memories? I feel uncomfortable with you, but that might change once we get undressed and get in bed?"

He couldn't hide the smile on his face. He was finally one step closer to destroying his brother. He would never forgive Katie once she made love to him.

"Really? You want to make love?" He acted dumbfounded as though he couldn't see the hurt in her eyes.

"Yes, but only if you truly believe that you will get your memories back?"

He helped her to her feet. "I do believe it is a good start. I have to feel connected to you and this is the best way to do that."

She put on a fake smile and let him walk her to the room. The kids were still asleep so they wouldn't know anything was going on. Once inside the room, he immediately began tugging at her clothes and she stopped him. "Slow down."

"I am sorry. We can go as slow as you would like." He gently kissed her lips.

It had just started raining and the sound of raindrops hit the top of the room. It was quite gloomy, but at the same time set a romantic mood for the two of them. Katie focused on the sound of the rain and imagined the way it use to feel when Jase would make love to her. It was always passionate and crazy, warm and sweet. She could remember the scent of his skin on her after they had just got done. The smell of his cologne would linger on her skin for hours.

Ethan removed her shirt, exposing the mounds of her breasts. He slowly dropped her bra straps below her shoulders and began kissing her bare skin that was hidden beneath the straps. "I have needed this."

Katie ran her fingers through his dark, smooth hair. She always loved teasing his hair. It was like velvet to her. She felt her bra drop to the floor. A piercing sensation tingled in her breasts as she felt the warmth of his tongue against her hard nipples. She let out a moan which drove him wild.

His lips traveled from her breasts to her neck. He could hear the blood pumping through the veins in her neck.

It was more arousing to know that the blood was moving so fast because she was turned on by his touch. For a moment he forgot why he was there and what he was up to. He caught a glimpse of her scent in her hair. It smelled of roses. She had a hint of lavender on her skin and he could smell her sex with his vampire senses. Everything was heightened to him. He could imagine how wet she was for him. She had to be dripping for him.

He tugged her pajama bottoms off and was pleased to find that she wasn't wearing any panties. He sent a trail of kisses from her neck down to the start of the dark, coarse hair above her vagina. His gaze locked on hers as he slowly dipped a finger inside of her. She trembled with delight. She wanted more. She was craving the man she so desperately loved.

He stuck another finger inside of her as she lifted her left leg and draped it over his shoulder. She wanted more. A loud thunder cracked across the sky, making her jump, but he didn't stop. He pressed his fingers harder inside until she couldn't take standing anymore. He then stood up and pushed her onto the bed. She laughed as she bounded down.

"I want you so bad!" He growled deep into her ear.

She stared at him with hungry lust in her eyes. The look sent him into a power drive. He flipped her over onto her knees and grabbed her by the hair. He began licking her from the center of her back up to her neck. He wanted to bite her. He had to taste her blood. His fangs came out and she could feel his breath on her skin and had goosebumps run down her body. He was just about to bite her when something smashed into their house.

"What was that?" She panicked as she grabbed her robe.

"It was nothing. Come back to bed." He reached for her hand.

She slapped his hand away and ran downstairs to check on the baby and Michael. She looked inside their rooms and they were still sound asleep. She felt better knowing that they were ok. When she made it to the kitchen, she noticed her door was open. The winds outside were so strong that the windows were rattling. She was struggling to push the door close.

Ethan made his way down and helped her close the door. Katie took it as a sign that something wasn't right. She was glad that she didn't make love to him. She may have been in the moment, but something didn't feel right and she would have made a huge mistake if she hadn't stopped.

Ethan grabbed her by the waist. "Let's go upstairs and finish what we started."

She was hesitant. She didn't want to. "Jase let's wait until tomorrow. That has me shaken up."

He could hear her heart beating so he knew that she was lying, but he had to pretend that he believed her. "That is fine Beautiful. We will finish what we started in the morning." He kissed her cheek.

Katie went into the room and checked on her children once more before returning to bed. She noticed that she had a missed call from Jackson on her phone.

"Jase, I will be upstairs in just a few. I missed a call from Jackson."

"It's the middle of the night. Surely he can wait until the morning."

She felt like he was suggesting that she cared more about Jackson than him. "Exactly, something could be wrong with Saide or their baby." She rolled her eyes.

Ethan walked past her and walked to the front door.

"Where are you going?" She was curious.

"To stay with Derek. My sister is still missing and he
needs me. I will be back in the morning." He left without
even a kiss.

She didn't have time to worry about that right now. No
matter how much it killed her on the inside, she had to
stay strong. She called Jackson to see what he had
wanted.

"Katie?" He answered. "Please tell me that Sadie is with
you?"

Katie's heart ran cold. "No, she isn't. I'm sorry."


"The Nanny said that she left earlier today and no one
has seen her all day. This isn't like her." He worried.

"Have you tried calling her? Maybe she is at the store?"

"She isn't. I am telling you. Something is wrong and she
has been hallucinating. I think she might be sick and
wandered off." He grew quiet for a moment. "What if
Jessica found her? She could be in real danger."

Katie tried keeping him calm, but now she was also
skeptical. He could be right. This has happened before.
She felt a burning sensation in her lungs. It was hard to
breathe. She could never handle it if anything happened
to Sadie. She was the only real thing she had in her life
these days, other than her children.

"Katie? Are you there?"

Jackson's voice broke through the silence that
surrounded her. "Yes, I'm here. Jackson, I don't know
what to do. Maybe she will be back soon. Call the police
and they can search for her. I will be on a plane first
thing in the morning and I will help you look for her."

"No, you have Michael and Athina. If she isn't here
come morning, I am sending out a search party."

"Keep me posted." She hung up.

She tried calling Sadie several times without an answer. She would go to voicemail every time. It was going to be a long night and she had to face it alone.

She went upstairs after locking up the house and she lay in bed thinking of everything she was going through. She was worried about her friend and Jase. She was also worried about what would happen to her children if their father never remembered her again. Her heart felt so heavy with pain and grief. Her life was no longer normal, but maybe it never had been. The pain was so bad that she had a hard time dealing with it and tonight she needed someone to hold her and the two people she needed more than anything were gone. She rolled over in the bed and looked at a photo of her and Jase on their wedding day. It brought tears to her eyes.

*"Jase, where are you? I feel like you are a shell of who you once were. We are so far away from each other, even when we are in the same room." She had a tear fall. "I miss you so much. I just want us back."*

She needed Jase more than anything. He was always the one that she could count on when she couldn't run to Sadie. She picked up her phone one more time and dialed Sadie's number. This time after three rings someone answered, but didn't speak a word.

"Sadie? Are you there?" Katie sat up.

All she could hear was static and heavy breathing. "Sadie? Please let me know if you are okay? "

Finally, a voice spoke, but it was hard to hear and distorted. "Sadie is ok. She is not in danger, but you are. I am coming for you. I will keep you and your kids safe."

She didn't say anything. She could hardly make out what this person was saying and she didn't know who it was.

"Katie, you can't trust Jase."

She heard that loud and clear. "Who is this? Do you have Sadie?"

"Sadie is fine. Jase is not what he seems. He is a
monster." The warning was coming through louder.

"Who is this?"

"I can't say. You won't believe me unless you see me.
Just be warned. You can't trust Jase."

She was getting worried. Why does he keep telling her
to not trust Jase?

"Jessica? Is that you?" She wondered.

"No... I am a friend. I will be coming for you tomorrow.
Stay away from Jase."

They hung up. Katie was even more worried now that
she spoke to this weird person on Sadie's phone. She
believed that Sadie might be safe, but why didn't they
want her to trust Jase? What was going on? Was she in
danger? She knew that she would be up all night. There
was no way that she could sleep knowing that her life
could be in danger.


    Ethan got back to Derek's to find him sitting at the
table looking through some files from the police
department. He had a stern look on his face and he was
very concentrated, so much so that he didn't realize
that he was there. "Is everything ok?" Ethan wondered.

Derek looks up at him for a moment. "Your friend,
Dave... He is missing."

Ethan knew that he had to act concerned. He knew that
if anyone grew suspicious of him that it was over. "He
might just be out on a case."

"No, they have footage of someone going into his room
and never saw anyone leave. When they went back
inside all the files were gone and there were signs of a
struggle."

Ethan was worried. He was concerned that they saw who entered the room to his motel on the footage. "Did they get a good look at the guy?"

"No, they are analyzing it, but it will take a couple of days to get it back.

*"Good, I have time to go to the station and find the tape." He thought to himself.*

"Jase? Why are you here? I thought you were making up with Katie?" Derek was curious as to what he would say.

"Oh, well we decided to wait until tomorrow, but I think I am going to postpone that. Something came up that I have to deal with tomorrow."

Derek was puzzled by that statement. "And this is more important than your wife?"

*"Damn it! He is on to me. I need to think fast."*

"No, I am doing this for her. It is a surprise. Just something to help us rekindle our love."

Derek didn't believe him. He felt more was going on than what Jase was telling him. He knew not to push the issue because he knew that Jase was in a fragile state of mind.

"I am going to get some rest. You should as well and then we can begin our search for my sister again." Ethan walked away without another word.

Derek watched as he walked away not sure what was going on since they hadn't even started searching for Rebecca. Jase was too different since the wreck. He would never be so calm about his sister being kidnapped. It just did not make sense to him. How could he be this calm?

Once Ethan made it up to his room he called Jessica who was asleep. "Hello" She rubbed her eyes.

"How are Jase and Rebecca?" He asked.

"Why are you calling? It is the middle of the night. Some of us need to sleep." She looked at the time on the clock.

"Remember who is in charge. You do as I say whenever I say." He demanded. "Now go downstairs and check on them."

Jessica hesitated for a moment before putting her slippers on and making her way down to the basement. She hated going down there by herself. It gave her the creeps. She unlocked the door and slowly went inside. It was dark and quiet. Jase and Rebecca were a little too quiet. She flipped the light switch on and was shocked to see that Jase was no longer sitting in the chair that he was tied to. She turned to find him standing behind her and without a word he grabbed her and sunk his teeth into her neck. She struggled to get free, but his strength was beyond anything human. She drug her feet across the floor and he continued sucking the blood from her vein.

Rebecca could hear noises coming from the other side of the room, but she couldn't tell what was going on. "Jase? Is everything ok?" She worried.

His eyes were glowing red and he was still hungry. He needed more blood. He continued nursing on her neck until her body went limp in his arms. He knew at this moment she was almost dead. "Jase? What's going on?" Rebecca cried out.

Jase pulled himself together and pulled away from Jessica leaving her lifeless on the cold basement floor. He backed away and sat idol on the floor away from her. He was in shock. What has he become? What did Ethan do to him and why?

Jase looked over at Rebecca who still could not see through the potato sack on her head. He made his way to her and pulled the bag from her face. "Jase?" She focused on the blood leaking from his mouth. "You're bleeding."

"It's not my blood." He walked over around her and broke the chains that had her locked to the chair.

Rebecca was floored by him being strong enough to break the chains. "How did you do that?" She wondered as she stood up from the chair.

"We don't have time to talk. We have to get out of here."

Jase grabbed her hand and quickly exited the room. Rebecca could not make sense of what was going on. She saw Jessica lying half-dead on the floor and now her brother had superhuman strength. She had to focus on escaping and getting back to Derek. He had to be so worried about her. As they ran past a room, they could smell a strong odor coming from inside.

Rebecca gagged as the odor hit her in the face like a ton of bricks. She covered her nose with her hand. "What is that smell?"

Jase opened the door and looked inside. His heart sank as he saw Dave, lying on the floor decomposing. "Dave?" Jase ran to him.

Rebecca grabbed his hand tighter. "We have to go. He is gone."

She could see the tears rolling down his cheek. Dave and Jase had been friends for years. They were like brothers. She managed to help pull him away from the door and they made it out of the house. Now they had to figure out where they were and how to get home.

## Chapter 9

Sadie was getting bored just sitting around with no one to talk to and nothing to do. She couldn't just sit around waiting to know if her friends were safe. She just got Michael back in her life and she was not about to lose him again. She got dressed and called a cab to get her so that she could hurry up and get to Katie's and try to help her. She had to know the kind of man that Jase really was before it was too late. She got in the cab and headed towards Katie's.

Morning came fast and Katie was still upset about what Jase had done the night before. He didn't even try to come home or call and say that he was sorry. She felt that he was a completely different person and that maybe it was time for her to move on. She had to accept her new reality and that was that her husband was gone.

Katie sat at the table still confused by the phone call she received the night before. Someone was warning her about Jase. She knew he had changed, but didn't feel threatened by him until now. She wasn't sure if she should be concerned about having him around her children or not. He had never tried hurting them and he was still a good father. Katie looked up when she caught a glimpse of someone looking through her kitchen window. She slowly walked over to take a peek, but no one was there. *"Get it together, Katie...You are losing your mind."*

Katie jumped when a knock came at her front door. She told Michael to stay in his room until she knew who was at the door. She was not expecting company.

The knock grew louder as she made her way to the door. She felt relieved when she saw that it was just Jase.

"Jase? You scared the hell out of me." She pulled the door open.

He had a movie in his hands and a smile on his face. "I am sorry, Beautiful."

She looked at the movie. It was one of her favorites. "A Walk to Remember?" She smiled. "You hate that movie."

"Yeah well... I love you, so this is my way of apologizing."

Michael ran out of his room and ran towards Jase. "Daddy!" He hugged Jase tightly.

Ethan knew that he had the kids fooled, but wasn't sure how his performance was going for Katie.

"Hey, there little man." Ethan hugged him tightly.

"Can I come inside?" Ethan wondered.

She nodded as she pulled the door open for him to enter.

Sadie was finally about to arrive at Katie's house but was stopped by Michael who was standing outside the gate of her home. She climbed out of the car and approached him, unsure of why he was just standing there. "Michael? What are you doing?" She asked.

"I could ask you the same thing. I told you to stay put." He snarled at her with a glow in his eyes.

She felt a little uneasy and worried that he might attack her. He saw the fear in her eye and he composed himself. "I am sorry, but you have put all of you in danger. Jase is inside and if you say anything, Katie and her children are in danger. You can't go in there."

"But Michael, we have to do something. We can't just sit back and let Jase hurt them."

"We won't, but you can't be here." He took her arm and walked her back to the cab.

"Get your hands off of me. That is my friend and I am going to help her stay safe." She pulled her arm back.

"Is everything ok?" The cab driver asked.

Sadie looked at Michael and then at the cab driver. "Everything is fine."

Michael walked her over to the gate. "I can see we are not going to resolve this, so I have a plan and if we work together we can at least get the children to safety."

Sadie listened intensively as Michael explained what to do. He had a plan and she was willing to do whatever it took to save her friend and the children. Michael ordered the driver to wait for them to return with the children. He explained to Sadie that they would have to help Katie next, but that they couldn't let on that they knew Jase was the bad guy this whole time.

Katie and Jase were sitting on the couch trying to talk things out while Michael was watching TV in his room and Athina was sleeping. Once more a knock came at the door.

"I will be right back. " Katie smiled at Ethan as she walked to the door.

She was amazed to see Sadie standing on the porch. She grabbed her and hugged her. "What are you doing here? Jackson is worried sick about you!"

"I was trying to surprise you guys. I called Jackson, he had forgotten that I told him that I was coming in for a visit." Sadie lied.

Katie was happy that her friend was back in town. 'is everything ok?"

"Yes, I was actually hoping I could take Michael to the park today. I could take Athina as well so you and Jase can catch up?"

Katie looked back at Jase, still feeling uneasy around him.

"Unless something is going on and in that case, I am sorry that I interrupted."

Katie took Sadie by the hand and walked her inside. "Don't be silly. We are fine. Of course, you can take the children to the park."

"Great." Sadie was trying not to show her hidden agenda on her face.

Ethan stood up and walked over to the ladies. "Hey, Sadie. How are things going?"

She began to tremble and her heart was racing. She had to try and compose herself or their plan would become void. If he found out they were on to them, he would kill them all. She cleared her throat. "Everything is fine. I just wanted to spend some time with my niece and nephew today."

Ethan studied her face for a moment. She was rather pale and didn't look well. *"Was she keeping something?"*

"Hmmm... Are you ok? You seem off?" He noticed.

*"Shit! He knows!"* She was relieved when she saw Katie with Michael and Athina.

"Bye, daddy!" Michael hugged Ethan.

Ethan grinned as he hugged his son. Katie was putting Athina in her stroller and grabbed her diaper bag from the closet. "This should be everything."

"Oh, I was hoping I could keep them overnight in my hotel?" Sadie blurted out.

Katie was growing suspicious. "What? Hotel? You can stay here. We have plenty of room." Katie suggested.

"As I said, you and Jase have some things to deal with and it is better if you guys have some privacy. Don't you agree, Jase?"

Ethan was weary of her intentions but agreed with her anyway. If she was keeping something from him, he would find out sooner or later. "I agree with her. We could watch the movie I brought and reminisce and try to rekindle some of our past?"

Katie walked over and grabbed extra diapers and formula for Athina. "This should get her through the night." Katie kissed Michael and Athina and hugged Sadie before they all left.

Once Sadie and the children left, Ethan walked Katie back over to the couch so that they could watch the movie. This time he would be on his best behavior so that he would get back on her good side.

Derek was at home trying to come up with a way to find Rebecca. He felt as though the police department was not doing enough and now with Dave missing, he was on his own. He flipped through files reading one page after another and could not come up with a simple answer. He knew Jessica was behind all of this. He just had to find her.

Just then Rebecca and Jase barged in through the front door. Derek was startled and ran towards them.

"Rebecca?" He was in shock. "How? Are you ok?" He hugged her.

"Yes, I am fine. I am worried about Jase." She tried to catch her breath.

Jase was weak and doubled over in pain. He had sweat pouring from his face and his skin was pale and clammy.

Derek was confused. He had just been with Jase a few short hours ago. How could he be in this bad of shape? Derek helped get him to the couch so that he could rest.

"What happened?"

"Derek, I know this is a lot and that you have a lot of questions, but right now we have to help him."

"How? I don't even know what is wrong?"

"He needs blood." She announced.

"Then we need to get him to the hospital, but I don't see where he is losing blood."

"No sweetie, he needs blood... to feed off of." She looked at him with a blank expression on her face.

He moved away from Jase and walked over to Rebecca. "Honey, you are not making sense. What did Jessica do to you?"

"I need you to trust me on this one. Nothing is what it seems. Jase is a vampire."

Derek stood there shocked. He didn't know what was going on or why Rebecca was saying the weird stuff that she was saying, but he knew they both needed medical help right away.

"How about we get you both to the hospital?"

All of a  sudden Jase leaped off of the couch and pushed Derek against the wall. Derek was mortified when he was Jase and his gleaming red eyes and sharp, pointy fangs. "Now do you believe her?"

Rebecca grabbed Jase by the arm. "Let him go Jase."

Jase loosened his grip and walked back to the couch.

"Look, Derek... Whatever Jessica did to him, she wasn't alone. Ethan, our brother was involved. He did this to him."

Derek pulled himself together. "How is this real? Are you one as well?"

"I don't think so. I mean I haven't craved blood." She answered.

"She has to taste human blood to trigger it. Ethan fed me blood. That is how he was able to change me." Jase spoke in a strong but weak voice.

"So what do we do? Are you going to kill us since you are now a blood-hungry monster?" Derek was fearful for his life.

"It isn't like that! Nothing you see on TV is real! Except I now live forever until someone decapitates my head. Stakes, holy water, garlic, and sunlight are all myths. I don't know everything, but I know I need blood to keep my strength up."

"What can I do?" Derek wondered.

"Honey, you work at the hospital. We need you to steal some blood for him."

"What? You can't be serious? People are dying, they need that to live."

"But Jase will die if he doesn't get it. Either way, you would be saving a life."

"He is a monster... He hardly qualifies for a blood transfusion."

Rebecca pleaded with him. "Please, he is my brother and the only family I have left. Do it for Katie and her children as well."

He thought for a moment. He could never say no to her. Those soft brown eyes always broke down his walls. "Ok, but I can only do it this time. After this, you will have to figure it out."

"Deal!" Jase agreed through the abdominal pain.

Derek left to go get the blood.

"I can't believe that I drink blood now." He rolled over to grab the phone.

"Who are you calling?" Rebecca asked.

"Katie. She has to know we are ok."

Rebecca yanked the phone from his hand. "Absolutely not! If he is with her, then that puts her in even more danger. We have to go about this differently."

He knew that she was right. He didn't even try arguing with her. He was in too much pain.

"Jase, try and get some rest. Derek shouldn't be too long. Besides, how hard could it be to steal a couple of pints of blood?" She made a joke.

Jase chuckled through the agonizing pain before he slowly drifted off to sleep.

Ethan and Katie finished watching the movie and decided to sit in the kitchen with a glass of wine. They tried talking about all the memories they made in hopes that something would trigger just one memory.

"You're beautiful." He noticed the way the light flickered in her eyes.

Katie blushed as she took another sip of wine.

"Do I make you uncomfortable?"

"No, it is just that you haven't called me beautiful in a long time. It is nice."

I reached across the table and caressed her hand. "It won't always be this way. I feel like I am getting close to remembering."

"You're worth the struggle. I told you that I will always fight for you and our love." She smiled.

Ethan actually forgot for a moment that he was pretending to be Jase. He could see why Jase was in love with her. Unfortunately, he was the evil twin, that no one was ever going to love and he was going to make sure it stayed that way. He did enjoy pretending to be Michaels and Athina's father. He was never around children and he could never hurt a child. He knew they were innocent and if Katie would love him the way she loved Jase, they could be a happy family.

Derek was finally on his way back from the hospital with the blood. He stole a whole cooler full and knew if anyone suspected him, he would be without a job. He had thought to turn around several times and put it back before anyone had noticed, but then he thought about how disappointed his wife would be and he could not let her down. He would do anything to keep her happy.

He grabbed his phone so that he could let Katie know about Rebecca and Jase.

Katie saw that Derek was calling, but she pushed it to her voicemail. She wanted to focus on her night with Jase.

"Who was that?" Ethan grew curious.

She rested her phone on the counter. "It was Derek. I will call him in a little while."

"Are you sure? It may have been important?"

"He will leave a message if it is."

He got up, walked over to her, and kissed her cheek. "I am going to run to the restroom. I will be right back."

Ethan called Jessica from the other room. She was just waking up from the blood loss she endured from Jase. "Hello?" She spoke in a faint voice.

"How are our guests?" He was curious.

Jessica tried pulling herself up. She was weak and could barely move. She looked around and noticed that they were gone. "We have a problem."

Ethan didn't like the sound of that. "What do you mean?"

"They are gone."

"Gone? What? How the hell did that happen?" He was furious. He knew if they got away they would spoil his plans.

"Jase broke out of the chains and he bit me and drained me of a lot of blood and left me for dead."

"Do you think I care? How could you be so stupid? If anyone finds out about me then my plans are over. They win."

Jessica pulled herself up and sat in the chair. She was still bleeding from her neck and she was sore. "Am I a vampire now?"

"Honey, you wish... But you will pay for allowing them to get away. You might want to run and never look back." He hung up.

Katie decided to listen to the message that Derek left on her voicemail.

*"Katie... Jase and Rebecca are back home and safe. I am not sure how Jase found her but they are here. Jase is ill, but I will take care of him for you and send him home soon. Call me when you get this message."*

Katie was confused by his message. What did he mean? Jase is fine. He is here with me. She picked the phone up and immediately called Derek back.

"Derek? What do you mean Jase is with you guys? He is here and he is fine?" She questioned him.

"That isn't Jase. That is his twin brother Ethan. You need to get out of that house now!" Derek demanded.

No sooner than the words left his lips, she was interrupted by Ethan. "Is everything ok?"

She lost the feeling on her lips and couldn't find the words to respond back. Her heart pounded in her chest and her mind was blank. She kept playing over and over again all the things that were signs that this was not her husband. He walked closer to her and she took a step back. Ethan noticed the change in her. She knew.

"Katie? Are you there?" Derek was worried.

Ethan took the phone from her hand. "Derek, she will call you back."

Katie slowly backed up away from her. He just smiled as he walked with her. "What's wrong baby? Don't you love me?"

"Stay away from me!" She hollered out in fear.

She backed up until the wall was pressed firmly against her back. Ethan continued to follow her until his chest was almost touching hers. She couldn't catch her breath as she trembled with fear. She couldn't focus on anything, but this man was standing in front of her looking identical to her husband. She had no idea. Jase never told her about his brother. It explained a lot but how did he pull this off and why didn't she catch on sooner?

"What's the matter? I thought you wanted to fight for me?" He mimicked her words back to her.

"You are not my husband!" She smacked at him, but he grabbed her wrists firmly and held them against the wall.

"That is true, but that doesn't mean that I don't have feelings for you." He admitted.

"Feelings? Seriously? If you have feelings for someone, you don't parade around town pretending to be someone else."

"But surely my brother mentioned me. I wouldn't think that he would keep a secret this big?" Ethan played off of her emotions.

She knew that he was right. Why did he keep this a secret? Didn't he love her enough to share everything with her?

Ethan lowered her hands down and moved a strand of her hair and tucked it behind her ear. "You are absolutely beautiful. I can see why my brother was in love with you."

"Don't touch me!" She brought her knee up and kneed him right in his manhood.

He backed up and fell to his knees in pain. While he was down she kicked him in the face knocking him over as she ran towards the door. Just as she got to the door, Ethan grabbed her by the hair and slung her across the room. She hit her head on the coffee table and passed out.

# Chapter 10

Derek made it back to Jase and Rebecca who were just sitting on the couch awaiting his return. "We have to hurry. Ethan knows that Katie knows who he is and she is in danger!" Derek barged through the doors with the cooler in his hands.

Jase sat up quickly. He dropped instantly from being so weak. "How did he find out?"

"I am sorry. I wasn't thinking and I called her to let her know that you guys were ok and Ethan overheard us. He hung the phone up and I am scared to think that he may have hurt her." Derek placed the blood in front of Jase.

Jase began drinking from one of the blood bags and he could feel his veins coming to life and his hunger was becoming satisfied. He felt rejuvenated and ready to go. His mind was fueled with rage and anger and he was ready to take his brother out of this world. He flew off the couch and made his way to the door.

"Jase! Slow down!" Rebecca yelled out of concern.

Jase turned to face her. "No one hurts my wife and gets away with it. I will be back once he is dead!"

"Jase? He is our brother and he obviously has some serious mental issues. We can help him become a better person." Rebecca pleaded with him as her eyes became heavy with sorrow.

Jase turned to face her. He could feel her pain so strong that it was hurting him, but he knew that Ethan wouldn't change and that he would continue to pursue them if he wasn't killed. "Rebecca, I am sorry, but this is the only way it will end." He kissed her cheek and left.

Derek tried to comfort Rebecca the best way he knew how. He held her tightly in his arms and rubbed her back as she cried into his chest.

Ethan walked over to Katie who was passed out on the floor with blood dripping from her head. He leaned over to lift her in his arms and ran his finger through the blood on her head and sucked it from his finger. "Mmm... Delicious." He growled as he lifted her in his arms.

He opened the door to leave and Michael was standing there. "Going somewhere?"

Ethan smirked at him. "Get out of my way."

Michael wouldn't budge. "Put her down and we can handle this monster to monster." His eyes turned red as blood and as bright as fire. His teeth were now fangs and there was the urgency to rip Ethan's heart from his chest.

"Don't be stupid. You are no match for me. I made you the monster that you are." Ethan pushed his way through.

Michael grabbed jumped back in front of him stopping him from getting to his car.

"I have a trick for you. Something only I can do to you since I turned you. It is kind of fun actually. Watch this. " He said with an evil smile on his lips. "Don't... Move."

Michael laughed as he tried to take a step closer. He couldn't move. He was under some type of compulsion. "What did you do to me?"

"Don't worry, you will be able to move in an hour. You see in a sense I am your master. You have to do everything I say, including killing Sadie if I so choose, so I would stay on my good side."

This began to worry Michael. He wouldn't be able to handle it if anything ever happened to Sadie. He was aching on the inside, knowing that he had to back down as he watch Ethan place Katie in the car. His feet were glued to the ground. He couldn't help her no matter how hard he tried.

"I will catch you later." Ethan taunted him once more as he got in the car and sped away.

Michael couldn't do anything, but watch them drive away into the dark.

It wasn't long before Jase pulled up. He saw Michael standing in the driveway. He was shocked and a little mortified by what he was seeing. "How could this be happening?" He rubbed his eyes.

"Jase? How did you get back here so soon and what did you do to Katie?" Michael was worried when he didn't see Katie in the car.

"Michael? I thought you were dead." Jase walked over to him.

"What? It is your fault I am this monster! Free me now!" Michael demanded.

"Wait... Michael. I am Jase. I have a twin and he is behind all of this. He is trying to take over my life." Jase began to explain.

Michael thought about it for a moment. "If this is true then Katie is in a lot of trouble because he has her," Michael confessed.

Jase ran into the house looking for the kids. No one was there. He ran back out to Michael who was still standing in the same spot. "Where are my kids and why are you just standing there? I need your help."

"The kids are fine. They are hidden away with Sadie and as far as me moving I still have about 45 minutes before I can move. Your brother ordered me to stay here and because he was the one that turned me, I have to do everything he says." Michael spoke with annoyance in his voice.

"Damn it!" Jase kicked the dirt. "This just keeps getting better."

"Go find them. I will be right behind you." Michael encouraged him.

"What about you? I hate to just leave you here like this."

"I will be fine. Just go find her. I believe he is taking her to his mansion up by the lake in east Chattanooga. Be careful. You may be super-human now, but you can still be killed."

Jase looked up at him as he walked over to his car. "Thanks, man. I am glad that you are back." Jase got in his car and drove away to find his wife.

Jase drove faster than he had ever driven before. His mustang did not disappoint when it came to speed. He must have run every red light there was. Nothing was going to stop him from getting to Katie.

Michael was able to move after the hour was up. No sooner than he began to move a car pulled up. Jessica got out of the car and froze when she saw Michael walking toward her. She slowly backed up towards her car as he walked closer to her. "Let me explain." She held her hands up in surrender.

"Explain?! It is because of you that I died and lost the woman I was going to marry!" He pushed her against the car knocking the air from her lungs.

"No! You don't understand!" She coughed. "It was him!" She sobbed. "I would never hurt my daughter."


He let her go and tried to let her talk. He was so enraged by this lady. So much hate was felt for her.

"Ethan had me under some type of spell or something. He controlled everything I was doing and now I am in danger because Jase and Rebecca got away. I just had to see my daughter one last time before I ran and never came back." She cried.

 Michael wanted to believe her, but he still saw an evil lady standing before him as she pulled the trigger that ended his life.

"Please, you have to believe me. I am so sorry. I never wanted to hurt anyone. I don't know why I couldn't stop him or myself."

"It is too late. Ethan has Katie and I am on my way to help Jase rescue her." He admitted.

"I will go with you." She offered.

"Are you a vampire as well?"

"No, I am human."

"Then it is too dangerous for you. You will only get in the way." He shot her offer down.

"Michael? She is my daughter. If anything I could be bait. I could buy you some time." Jessica begged for his mercy.

 Michael thought for a moment. She was right. If he was going to save Katie, it wouldn't hurt to have someone there to use as bait. It didn't sound good, but Katie didn't deserve this life she had been given and Sadie would never forgive him if he didn't save her friend.

"Fine, but if you so make one wrong move, I promise, I will make your death as slow and agonizing as possible. Do you understand?" He threatened her in his most intimating voice.

She just nodded her head as she got in the car.

Ethan grabbed Katie from the backseat of his car and carried her into his Mansion. The blood had dried on her head and she was still passed out. He placed her on the sofa that was in his living quarters and gave her a gentle shake. "Wake up sleeping beauty."

She slowly opened her eyes. Her head was aching and her vision was a little hazy. The room was spinning and she didn't know where she was.

"Katie? Everything is ok." Ethan assured her.

"Jase?" She cleared her throat.

She looked over at Ethan and in her mind, she believed it was truly Jase.

"Not quite." He giggled.

It hit her like a ton of bricks all at once. "Ethan?!" She sat up quickly and nearly fell off the sofa. "Where am I? What have you done?"

She panicked as she realized she had no idea where she was and she didn't know if anyone would find her.

Ethan walked closer to her and she scooted further back on the sofa. "Stay away from me!" She demanded.

He leaned in and placed a cold compress on her head. "Relax... I'm not going to hurt you."

She twitched when she felt the cold object on her wound. It sent a shocking pain through her head but felt good at the same time. "Ethan, why are you doing this?" She grabbed the compress from his hand.

"Because my brother and sister abandoned me when our mother was killed." He opened up.

For a moment she sat quietly unsure of how to handle the situation. She knew that if she wanted to survive that she would have to pretend to care. "I am sure they didn't mean to. They were just kids."

"So was I. I mean sure, I killed my own mother, and that probably scared the hell out of them, but they shouldn't hold that against me."

Her eyes widened hearing the truth spill from his lips. She couldn't believe what she was hearing. "Jase told me that he watched your father kill your mother."

Ethan began to laugh. "Really? And you believe that?"

"Why wouldn't I?" She responded.

"Just forget it! Everyone always believes Jase. He is a good child, but that is because he had put some mental block up that keeps him from remembering, but that will change."

She got up off the sofa and walked to him. "Tell me what happened?"

He looked at her trusting green eyes and for a moment he almost felt that he could trust her, but then he remembered that she was married to his brother.

"You must think I am a fool? No one will ever be trusted by me. Not Rebecca, not Jase, and most certainly... Not you." He walked over to his liquor cabinet and poured a glass of whiskey. "Drink this. It will help with the pain." He handed her the crystal goblet.

She took the whiskey and sipped on it. She wasn't much of a drinker other than having an occasional glass of wine.

He smiled watching her quiver from the overwhelming stoutness of the liquid courage in her glass.

"Why are you being so nice to me if you are just going to kill me anyway?" She questioned his agenda. "It doesn't make sense.

He came closer to her. "I honestly don't want to hurt you, but make no qualms about it, I will do whatever I have to and hurt whoever Jase loves, to bring revenge against my brother."

She gulped as he stood right before her. She felt like she couldn't move. He took the glass from her hand. "Do you know what I am?" He asked as he sipped from her cup.

She was confused."What do you mean?"

"I need you to stand still and remain calm as I show you who I really am."

She felt her body stiffen. It was like she couldn't move even though she wanted to. She was stuck and she felt mellow about it. "What's going on?"

"The whiskey you sipped from has my blood in it which enables me to compel anyone that drinks of it. I now control everything you do." He pulled the hair from her cheek and pushed it behind her shoulder exposing her neck.

"What is happening? What are you doing to me?" She wanted to cry but wasn't able to.

He could see the vein pulsating in her neck. He watched as it throbbed and flickered with every touch of his hand. "This vein right here looks appetizing." He ran his finger along it.

"Ethan? What are you doing?" She asked once more.

"Shhh... Don't be afraid of me. I will show you who I am and then you will understand what I am about to do next."

He was clearly talking in riddle because he was not making sense to her at all. He stepped away from her and slowly walked around her like a shark waiting out his prey. He came up behind her and slowly ran his hand along her hips and up her arms. "Don't be scared." He whispered against her ear. Then without warning he sunk his teeth into the vein that he had been admiring.

She could feel the pain of the bite and she couldn't move or stop him. It was like a pain she had never experienced. Her head began to spin and she couldn't feel her body anymore. She could feel her body being drained of her blood and she was fading. Once he saw that she had enough, he stopped sucking on her neck. Her body went limp in his arms and he carried her up to his room.

Jase finally pulled up to the mansion and quickly ran up to the door and kicked it in. "Ethan! Where the hell are you?" He hollered throughout the Mansion.

He ran through the entire place and there was no sign that he had even been there. They weren't here. He had tricked them. "Son of a Bitch!" He threw the table over in the living room.

Moments later, Michael and Jessica rolled up and came inside the mansion.

"Michael? I thought you said he would be here?" Jase stopped when he saw Jessica standing there.

Jase darted for her. He was so full of rage and he wanted to kill her before she had a chance to hurt anyone else. Michael leaped in front of her, keeping her from Jase's wrath.

"Whoa! Calm down and hear us out. She was under Ethan's spell this whole time. She didn't want to hurt anyone, but he compelled her to. She is just as much a victim as Katie."

Jase was still snarling at her with his blood-red eyes. He couldn't trust anything she said. "She is a liar! She has to die!"

"I am telling the truth!" Jessica scooted back.

"It sounds like a fabricated story if you ask me," Jase argued.

"Look, I understand that we have some major beef with her and we can deal with that later., but right now we have to work together to find Katie. There is no telling what Ethan has in store for her." Michael ranted. "She knows that if she messes up, there will be consequences."

Jessica didn't say another word. She knew that she was treading on thin ice.

Jase composed himself and backed away from her. Michael was right. All he cared about was saving his wife. They had to work together if they were ever going to find her. He just prayed that it wasn't too late.

"I remember him saying that he has several hideouts around Tennessee. I do believe he is still here, we just have to find out where he is hiding her and what his agenda is." Michael began working on a plan.

Jessica had remembered hearing Ethan talking about some of the plans he had for Jase. One, in particular, stood out. "He wanted Katie to fall in love with him." She began. "I told him that she was in love with Jase and that he didn't have a chance, but he refused to listen to a word I said."

This pissed off Jase even more. How could his own brother betray him this way? They were just kids, He didn't run away and leave Ethan to fend for himself. Katie had already been through so much. She didn't deserve this and the more he thought about her being left alone with Ethan, the more enraged he became. The thought of him touching her made him sick in his stomach.

"I know that this isn't what you want to hear, Jase, but for what it is worth, I don't think he wants to hurt my daughter, however, I do believe that he is planning on turning her." She stated.

"What?" Jase turned to face her with worry in his eyes. "Turn her?"

"Yes... That is his ultimate plan." She replied.

"How does that happen?" Jase asked not knowing he would not like the answer.

"Well, first she would have to be bitten twice. The first time, she would have to be almost completely drained and near death. Then once she heals from that bite, he would have to bite her again to complete the transformation."

"How long does that take to do?" Michael asked for Jase.

"About 3 days."

Jase hurled around and punched a hole through the wall causing Jessica to jump out of her skin. "How the fuck are we going to find her?!"

Michael walked over to try and ease his mind. He knew how much pain he was in. "Listen, it gives us three days to find her. That gives us a good amount of time to stop it and we don't know that he has even bitten her at this point, so there is still time which means there is still hope."

Jase looked over at Jessica who was fearful of his next reaction. She was the only human in the room and these two could turn on her at any given second.

"Relax... I am not going to bite you or kill you. Katie deserves to make that choice." He explained as he walked to the door of the mansion.

"Ok, so first thing first. We get a list of all the places he owns and we start from there." Michael began. "We have three days. Let's make them count."

# Chapter 11

Sadie was back at Michael's watching over little Michael and Athina. They played some games and watched a movie and she did whatever she could to keep their minds busy. They had no idea what was going on and she was going to make sure they never did.

She was so worried about Katie that having the children made it a little easier. She missed her daughter Anna and she knew that before long she would have to talk to Jackson and let him know that she wanted to be with Michael again. She didn't want to hurt him, but she knew that keeping it a secret would only hurt him worse.

Little Michael was yawning and falling asleep on the couch. She lifted him in her arms. "Let's get you in bed."

She laid him down in the bed and then checked on the baby that was sound asleep in the crib that Michael had bought, knowing that he was going to have them all stay there for safety. They both seemed so peaceful and happy and all she could think about was what happens if they can't save their mother this time.

The house was quiet and she felt so lonely. She hated not having someone to talk to or a way to call for help. She was away from everyone.

She heard a noise coming from outside and she quickly got up and walked to the door to see what it was. She was surprised to see Jase, Michael, and Jessica walking up to the door.

"What are they doing here?" She grew infuriated.

"We have a lot to explain and right now we all just need to go inside and talk. Keep it together Sadie." Michael ordered her like he was her master.

She was quiet and beside herself as she watched the three of them enter the house.

Michael explained to her about Jase having an evil twin and that Jessica was under Ethan's spell. He told her how they would all work together to make sure they find Katie and get her home safely to her children.

Jase sat down on the couch and buried his face in his hands and cried. Michael walked over and knelt in front of him on the floor. He rested his hand on his shoulder, "We will find her." He promised.

Jase looked up at him. His eyes were more blue than usual. His eyes were swollen with tears and his face was flushed and pale. "She thinks that I forgot how much I love her. What if something happens to her and she dies thinking I didn't love her anymore?"

"Jase, it is Katie. She knew something was off from day one. She even told me that she couldn't connect with him. I think she always knew somehow." Sadie tried to comfort him.

"She's right." Jessica horned in. "I know my daughter and she has always had a keen sense to bull shit. She can see right through people."

Jase shot a look her way. "Just like she did with Dylan? She couldn't tell he was a jackass."

"That was because she was blinded by love. He broke her down. There is no way that my daughter can't see through Ethan."

Jase dried his eyes. He knew he had to pull himself together.

"Can I please have a phone so I can call Jackson and check on my baby?" Sadie begged.

Michael knew she wanted to talk to Jackson more than check on the baby and he knew he had to back off and let her, no matter how much it pained him to do so. He handed his phone over to her. "You can use mine."

Sadie took the phone. She was a little awkward using his phone, but she had to make sure that they were ok.

"Hello?" Jackson answered.

"Jackson, it's me... Sadie." She replied.

"Sadie? Where the hell are you?! We have been worried sick about you." He stated.

"I am sorry. I came to be with Katie and help her with the kids."

"Seriously? You didn't even talk this through. I come home and find the nanny with our baby and you leave to be with Katie?"

"Yes, because she is in danger." She informed him.

He didn't say a word, but she could hear him breathing on the other end and she could tell he did not like her answer.

"Look Jackson, I will be home before you know it and we can talk then. I just wanted you to know that I am okay."

"What happened to you?" He finally spoke through the silence. "You are not the Sadie that I fell in love with."

"Yes, I am...

She was interrupted. "No, you aren't. The Sadie I fell in love with, would never have left her husband and child behind without saying a word."

"Jackson, my friend is in danger."

"And so if my wife and the mother of my daughter, but you didn't even stop to think about how this would affect us." He was frustrated and growing more irritable by the second.

"That isn't fair." She snapped back.

"Just forget it. Be careful. We will see you when you decide that we are more important than your friend that cries danger." He hung up.

Sadie handed Michael his phone and she could feel the whole room looking at her with sympathy in their eyes. She blinked back her tears. Michael held her hand, but she pulled away. "We should really get some rest. Tomorrow is going to be a long day. We don't have much time before Ethan changes her." She walked away leaving the room in silence.

It wasn't long before Michael joined her in his room. "I'm sorry that I got you in the middle of this." He spoke out as she sat down on the bed.

He walked over and sat down beside her. He could see so much pain and worry in her eyes and that was the last thing that he ever wanted to do to her. He was so in love with her that he would give up his life over and over again if it meant her living longer, even if it meant her never coming back to him.

"Sadie, I think that you should go home and be with your family. Jase and I will rescue Katie. You have a husband and a daughter that need you."

She looked at him with a lost look in her eyes. "What about what I want? Do you think that this is easy on me? I am married and have a child now, but you were the one that I was meant to be with, but you died and you left me and I moved on, but I never really moved on. I covered the pain and did what everyone wanted me to do. I love Jackson, but he isn't you." The tears flowed from her eyes down her cheeks.

Michael wrapped his arm around her. "It is ok. Let it out." He kissed her forehead.

"Michael, I love you. It is you I want to be with, but how do I walk away from a life that I brought a child into? I don't know what to do."

He took a deep breath and inhaled the smell of her hair. She always smelled of flowers. Sweet and crisp, like a breezy spring day. "A decision doesn't have to be made today. We will take it day by day and whatever happens, your daughter will not suffer. I promise."

She got out of the bed and walked around to stand in front of him. "Do you want me?" She asked. "Do you love me and want to be my husband?"

He pulled her down on his lap. "Honey, that is all that I have ever wanted. You are the only one for me and I will spend an eternity making sure that you know that."

She didn't say anything. Her face was long and weary. Thoughts were playing out in her head. They didn't have an eternity together. They had years. She would eventually die and he would continue to live on without her in his life.

"What's wrong sweety?" He played with her hair.

"Turn me..." She asked of him.

He didn't know how to respond. That isn't the life that he ever wanted for her or anyone else. It would rob her of so many dreams that she had. She would have an eternity of pain every time someone died. She had a daughter that needed a human mother. He couldn't even fathom the thought of taking her away from her child that way.

"I can't do that. You have a daughter. Your whole life would be changed forever."

She stood up. "None of that matters if I don't have you. How can I live a life that doesn't include you? I want us to be together forever, but that can't happen if I age and die. "She planted her lips against his. "Turn me... Let us be together for eternity." She began unbuttoning her shirt.

"But you have a daughter that needs you." He spoke in between kisses.

"She will have me... but I need you. I can't handle the thought of us not being together."

She sent soft kisses from his navel to his neck. "Please, Michael. I am begging you." She whispered against his ear.

He couldn't hide what she was doing to him. His erection was getting harder and throbbing to be in her. He wanted her so much and he wanted a life with her, but not like this. She didn't know what she was talking about. She was scared and not thinking rationally.

He grabbed her and pushed her away from him. "I can't do this." He admitted.

He hated seeing the pain that he inflicted on her. She was distraught and he was responsible for it.

"I don't understand... You said that you wanted me."
She gave him a dead stare.

"I do, but you are not thinking clearly. You have not had
enough time to process this."

"I have and I can't live without you again! I won't live
without you again!" She fell to her knees and began to
cry hysterically.

He walked over and tried pulling her up, but she
wouldn't let him. "No! You have no idea what I went
through! I can't lose you again!"

Jase walked in when he heard all of the commotion
coming from the room. He could actually hear her heart
breaking. Michael looked worried and more upset than
he had ever been.

"I can't do this. I have to get some air." Michael
stormed off and left Sadie sitting on the floor while she
was torn apart on the inside.

Jase followed after Michael while Jessica stayed with
Sadie. Jessica tried to help her up, but she grew angry
and pushed her. "Don't touch me!"

"Sadie, this isn't good. You have to pull yourself
together."

"That is easy for you to say! This is your fault! You are
the reason that Michael and I never got our happy ever
after! You killed him and because of that, you also killed
me!"

"I didn't know what I was doing... I was compelled to do
the things that I did. I would never hurt my daughter or
anyone else for that matter."

Sadie lifted herself off the floor and got close to Jessica
as if she was going to hit her. "I know that this may not
have been your fault, but every time I look at you all I
can see is the one who pulled the trigger on my fiance. I
can't erase what I remember or how I feel."

The words cut through Jessica like a knife. She could understand how Sadie felt. Ethan made sure that all of them were scarred for the rest of their lives and she was pretty sure that she had no chance to make it up to Katie either.

"I understand and I will forever do whatever I can to try and make it up to all of you. You will never know just how sorry I am who caused you this much pain, but right now at this moment, you have a choice to make before you hurt someone that you love just as much. You have a daughter and you owe it to her to do what is best for her."

Sadie wiped her cheeks dry and pulled herself together. "I love my daughter." She spoke softly.

Jessica reached out and pulled her into a warm embrace. "I know you do sweetie."

It was very quiet for a moment. Sadie got a look in her eye. She was a new person. "That is why I have to do what I am about to do."

Jessica wasn't sure what she was talking about, but as she pulled away she felt an excruciating sting in her back and fell to the floor.

Sadie had grabbed some scissors off the dresser behind Jessica and stabbed her in her spine. Jessica dropped to the floor. "I'm sorry, but if Michael won't turn me, I will find Ethan and get him to."

Sadie dropped the scissors on the floor and climbed out of the window and ran off before anyone knew that she was gone.

Derek and Rebecca had just shown up while Michael and Jase were outside talking. Rebecca ran over and hugged Jase.

"Thanks for meeting us out here. We needed someone to watch the children while we were gone." Jase admitted.

"Of course, but brother I am coming with you. Derek will watch the kids." She announced.

"No, most certainly not. If something happens, my children need two parents."

"Nothing is going to happen. The more of us that work together, the better our chances."

"Rebecca, we are vampires. We have the strength that no human alive can match."

Rebecca rolled her eyes at him. "I share the blood of both you egotistical morons."

"She has a point." Derek chimed in.

Jase looked over to Derek who seemed too calm. "You are supposed to be on my side."

"I am, however, I know her, and she will not listen to us and I know she is stronger than you think she is. She can handle this."

Jase paused when he began to smell a familiar smell. Michael also smelled it. "What's is that?" Jase asked.

"What? I don't smell anything." Rebecca stated.

"Blood." Michael acknowledged as he ran into the house back to where he left Jessica and Sadie.

Jessica was passed out on the floor as blood poured from her back. Jase turned as his eyes glowed red and his fangs became pronounced. He wanted to rip through her body and drain her of the blood that she was bleeding. It was warm and fresh and he knew it would satisfy his craving. He needed to feed on her vein.

Michael grabbed him and pulled him out of the room. "Get yourself under control."

"I just want a little bit." Jase tried to push his way back into the room.

"Jase! This is not you! This is Katie's mother."

Jase thought about Katie and slowly pulled himself together. He could never hurt Katie that way. He had to fight his urges. Michael could see that Jase was transforming himself back to look more human than a monster. He walked back into the room. Rebecca and Derek were huddled over Jessica.

"I am going to have to pull the scissors from her back, but I do, she will bleed out even more. She may not make it." Derek informed everyone.

"I can heal her." Michael walked over. "It is one of the many perks of being a vampire. All I have to do is drop a few drops of blood on the wound and it will heal from the outside in."

Derek began to yank the scissors from her back as Jessica began to wake up. She screamed out in pain. Michael bit his hand and let the blood drip into the open wound on her back. Jessica could feel a warming sensation fill the wound and she could feel her vessels healing and her tissue closing up.

Michael looked around noticing that Sadie was nowhere in sight. "Where the hell is Sadie?" He wondered.

Jase noticed that the window was open. "She had to go out the window. I am sure she just needed some fresh air after doing this. She will be back."

"No... She went to find Ethan." Jessica blurted out. "She is going to let him turn her."

Michael grew worried and anxious. He hit the wall beside him. "Damn it! What the hell is wrong with the women in this house!"

Jase grabbed him by the arm as he went to strike the mirror on the dresser. "She couldn't have gotten far. We can find her."

"We will all find her. Derek will watch the children and we will leave tonight." Rebecca offered.

Michael nodded as he tried composing himself. "We have to hurry. She could be in more danger than she realizes."

Derek walked over and kissed Rebecca. "Please be careful and come home safely to me."

Rebecca kissed him again. "You will never get rid of me that easy. I will always come home to you."

"You better." He hugged her.

"Let's go," Michael ordered.

They all grabbed some tools they needed to go up against Ethan and set out on a journey to find Sadie and Katie.

Sadie was out in the middle of nowhere. She didn't know the first place to look for Ethan or Katie. It was dark and creepy. She was a lady on foot in the middle of the woods. She hollered out for Ethan, but he wouldn't show up so she did the next best thing and cut her hand open hoping that the blood would draw him out and as she had hoped it had worked.

Ethan stood in the shadows of the trees staring at her with a grin on his face and a thirsty stare. "Either you are braver than you look or you have a death wish?"

"I want you to turn me." She stated out loud.

Ethan walked out of the shadows and walked toward her. "What makes you think that I would even want to turn someone like you?"

"It would hurt a lot of people like Katie and Jase for starters." She admitted.

He pulled her injured hand closer to his mouth. His eyes glowed and his fangs came down. "And why would you want to hurt your friend?" He wondered as he began to drink the blood from her hand.

His lips on her hand made her nervous, but she knew what she wanted. "Because if you turn me, then I can be with Michael for eternity."

Ethan giggled in the devilish giggle that he was famous for. Blood dripped from his bottom lip as he stared at her in her eyes. "It doesn't work that way, you silly girl."

She grew anxious and weary. Maybe she made a mistake trying to make a deal with the Devil himself? "I would live for eternity and I know that Michael loves me."

"Being a vampire changes you. You may not feel the same for him once you turn."

She didn't believe him. He had to be playing with her head. Michael and Jase both stayed true to who they were so why wouldn't she?

"Women are way more impulsive than men. When you change into a monster, you stop feeling the love you once felt. You can't handle that type of change. You may not even want Michael once you turn."


"Yes, I will. It will always be Michael. Please just turn me. He wouldn't do it and I can't live this life knowing that I can't be with him."

Ethan thought for a moment. "I will turn you. In fact, it would bring me great joy to turn Katie's best friend."

He pulled her close to him and stared into her saddened eyes for a moment. "This is going to hurt you more than it will hurt me." He didn't say another word. He bit down and sucked the blood from her neck until she fell limp in his arms.

Ethan continued sucking on her neck with a smile on his face as his eyes continued to glow. Without another thought, he swooped her up and they vanished into the darkness.

<br>

## Chapter 12

Morning came and Katie could feel the sunlight beaming in on her skin through the window of the room that she woke up in. She was in a huge, soft, bed with a thick velvet-like comforter. The room had a smell of an older type of home. Maybe Victorian style. She sat up in the bed, her head spinning. She was dizzy and a little nauseated from the night before.  She turned to look around and stopped when she felt a sharp pain in her neck. She ran her fingers along the holes that were left from Ethan biting her. She jumped when the door opened.

In walked Ethan. He was dressed in a white t-shirt and black jeans. He was grinning and looking at her with lust in his eyes. She was scared. She didn't know what was going on and why he had done what he did. Nothing made sense to her. She remained quiet as he sat down beside her. He ran his hand along her leg and she pulled herself away. He laughed under his breath.

"You may not want this yet, but soon you will." He promised her.

"I will never want you." She looked at him with great disgust.

"For now, before long it will be out of your control."

"What does that even mean? I am in love with Jase. He is my husband and the only man that I will ever love."

He stood up and smiled as he took a cup from her nightstand. He filled the cup with what looked like some type of fruit juice. It had a reddish tint to it. He handed her the glass.

"What is it?" She wondered.

"It is sex on the beach. I thought you might want something a little stronger today to help cope with everything."

She took a sip of the drink. It had a sweet, but bitter taste and it had a hint of irony in it, but it wasn't bad. She became very relaxed with just one sip and she wanted more. She gulped her drink down. She was drunk from just one drink. It had to be from the loss of blood. She felt as though she couldn't move and she was very calm when she should be panicked, but right now she didn't care. "What was in this?" She asked in a softened tired voice.

"That drink allows me to have control over you. I can now control everything that you feel and every move you make. That drink has my blood in it and when you ingest it, I can compel you." He grinned as he sat back down and took the glass from her relaxed hand. "I want you to remain calm."

All of a sudden, she felt like she couldn't move her body. She was aware of what was going on and she felt she could not stop it.

"I am going to turn you and you will become my pawn against my brother. Once you turn, you will do what I say at all times and you will kill my brother."

She wanted to yell, but she couldn't. She had to remain calm.

"I want you to kiss me." He leaned in pressing his lips to hers.

She couldn't stop it. She was kissing him back, even though she knew that it was wrong. What was he doing to her? Was he going to force her to make love to him? This would destroy her marriage. She felt him parting her mouth with his tongue and she was liking it despite how she felt. Do vampires have some type of sex appeal? She wondered to herself.

He stopped kissing her and stayed close to her face as he gazed into her eyes. "Tonight, we will finally make love. I am going to finally fuck you and make you forget all about Jase."

He laughed when he heard her heart skip a beat. He moaned against her lip. "I think you like the sound of that... Be honest with me." He compelled her once more. "Have you ever been fucked hard?"

She gulped. She didn't want to answer him but was not able to fight the urge to answer. " No." She blushed as she answered.

"From now on, you can not lie to me." He nibbled her bottom lip. "Have you ever wanted to be fucked hard?"

She nodded yes. Her skin was now burning with embarrassment. She wanted to scream and have him leave, but she couldn't.

"Mmm... Good girl." He teased. "Or should I say, bad girl? Do you like rough sex?"

"I don't know. I have never had rough sex." She blurted out.

"Are you satisfied with Jase in the bed?" He asked.

"Yes." She didn't hesitate.

He didn't like her answer. "How can you be satisfied if he doesn't fuck you the way you want to be fucked?"

"Because I love him. I will never love anyone the way that I love him." She answered once more.

Ethan grew annoyed and stood up. He started walking to the door stopping to look back at her. "Tonight, I will make sure you forget all about Jase. I will make you scream with pleasure." He winked at her, leaving her with an uneasy feeling in the pit of her gut.

Jase and Michael continued to search for Katie and Sadie. They so many places, but none of them were right. Jessica and Rebecca wandered off to ask people if they had seen their friends, but no one had.

"Man, this is all my fault. If I had just left Sadie alone, she would be home safe with her husband and daughter, but now she is with Ethan and she wants to become a vampire." Michael began to beat himself up.

Michael felt responsible for Sadie.  He didn't want this life for her, no matter how badly he wanted her. She would have to give up everything to be with him and that was a sacrifice that he was not willing to put her through.

"Michael? This isn't your fault. You were only trying to protect her. Sadie has never been happy since you died. She loves Jackson, but not as she loved you. I have watched her try to get over you and no matter what she did, she couldn't." Jase filled him in.

Michael frowned. He didn't like to think of her as being sad and lonely or even isolated from reality. "It just hurts." He kicked the dirt on the ground.

Jase gave him a friendly pat on the shoulder. "We will find them. And once we do, we will make it up to both of them."

"Yeah well, even if we find them, I have to let Sadie go."

Jase shot a sympathetic glance his way. He had no words to try to ease Michael's mind. He knew there was a storm brewing in his mind.

Rebecca and Jessica came out of the convenience store and met up with the guys.

"The cashier said that Ethan is a frequent customer. She said that he doesn't live too far, but can't ever seem to remember their conversations. We think that he must compel people around here." Rebecca stated.

"Maybe we could try and watch footage of the last time he was in here? We could see which direction he went." Jase wondered eagerly.

Jessica shook her head. "Nope, he took any footage that they had. We already tried."

Without warning a child about 10 years of age walked over to them. "Excuse me? I know Ethan."

Their eyes widened and their mouths dropped. This could be the break they had been looking for. Jase knelt in front of the little boy. "Can you tell us where he is?"

"Will he be in trouble?" The child asked as his eyes swelled with tears.

"What's your name?" Jase asked.

"Anthony."

"Anthony? That is a strong name. I love that name." Jase smiled. "Ethan has done some really bad things and he has my wife. If we don't find her and her friend soon, he might hurt them."

"But he is my friend."

Jase felt a lump in his throat and he had to fight to get words out. "I understand and we would never do anything to hurt Ethan. We just want our ladies' home with us. Please help us do that."

Anthony was quiet for a moment but then agreed to help. "He lives in the mountains in a secluded area. When it is dark, you cannot find it. I have been there a few times and it is really scary, but he is always really nice to me."

"Are we even talking about the same guy? Ethan is not a nice guy." Michael snapped.

Rebecca pushed him back and encouraged him to calm down. "He is just a child.

"He looks like you," Anthony told Jase.

"Oh come on... This could be part of his plan to lure us into a trap." Michael was growing angrier by the second.

Anthony began to shake as fear crept in. Jase took his hands to hold him steady. "It's ok. He is just scared and acting out. Can you take us to Ethan?"

Anthony agreed to help them. Jessica pulled Jase away for a moment. He leaned in and whispered to him. "He is just a child. We cannot put him in any danger."

Jase looked over towards Anthony and then back at her. "Unless you have a better plan I don't see any other way."

Jessica hated it, but she knew that he was right. "Fine, but you had better make sure nothing happens to him."

"I would never let anyone hurt a child." He agreed.

They all headed on their way to find Katie and Sadie. It was going to be a long ride so they were sure to stock up on supplies they would need. They had blood bags sitting on ice in the trunk for the vampires and snacks and waters for the ones that were still human.

Katie got out of the bed and searched the room for a way out, but bars were blocking the windows. She searched for a key to get out of the room and could not find one. She could hear, Ethan talking to someone out in the hall. It sounded like another man. She banged on the wall, hoping the man would hear her from inside the room. She paused when she heard footsteps growing nearer. She backed away from the door when she saw Ethan walk in with the man.

Ethan smiled at her and the man was unimpressed. "what's going on?" The man asked unknowingly.

"Well, because of Katie, you now have to die." Without warning, Ethan ripped into the man's neck.

Katie screamed and tried running, but Ethan grabbed her and threw her down on the bed. The man laid lifeless on the floor.

Katie smacked at Ethan and tried pushing him off of her, but she was no match for him. "Please don't hurt me." She cried.

Ethan smirked as he wiped her cheek. "I have bigger plans for us. I could never hurt you."

"Then let me go!" She demanded of him.

Ethan could hear her heart pounding faster in her chest. He could smell the saltiness of her tears and the scent of fear on her skin.

"Did you know that when you are scared that you put a scent out there that becomes like an erotic pleasure to vampires?" He licked his lips.

She didn't like the sound of that. She wanted him away from her.

"You are putting off such a strong scent right now and it is driving me crazy. I can feel my erection growing for you and it is hard for me to resist the urge to show you just how much I want you." He leaned down and kissed her cheek.

She pulled her face away. "Please don't do this."

He sat up and moved away from her. "I could never hurt the woman that I plan to spend my life with. By tonight, you will be all mine."

Her heart skipped a beat. She couldn't catch her breath. "I have children. They need me."

He laughed. "You silly lady. This is why I love you so much."

She was baffled. She was unsure of what he meant.

"I too have a child. A boy. He is 10 years old and if we are lucky, you will get to meet him soon."

The blood ran cold through her veins. How could he have a child? He isn't even technically alive.

"You're lying. "She called his bluff.

"Let me guess. You are one of the people who believe that vampires cannot conceive a child? With all of these myths about vampires, how could anyone ever know the truth?"

She sat up on the bed and pulled her legs up to her chest. She wanted to know the truth about vampires and how any of this is real. "Explain it to me then... I want to know all of your truths."

He giggled under his breath and rolled his eyes. "You could never handle all of the truth. Pay close attention to our eyes. They give away our mood. If our eyes are green, we are calm... Blue means we are sad or lost and red means we are angry. It is when we are angry that you should be more fearful of us. That is when we attack."

She studied his face. His eyes were already blue as were Jase's. "But you have blue eyes?"

"Our eyes will become so blue that they would look fake. They would almost look like the color of the bluest oceans." He continued explaining. He could see that she was eager to learn about his life.

"Go on... I am listening." She rested her hand on his.

He looked down at his hand. Feeling her warm silky touch on his skin awakened his inner human. "There is only one way to kill us and that is by severing our heads."

"So stakes don't work?" She was amazed.

"Why would they? We are technically dead." He laughed at the expression on her face. "Our hearts aren't truly beating so they are of no use to us."

She rubbed his arm softly allowing him to know that she cared. She didn't like the thought of anyone feeling alone. "So that is why you cannot love?"

She was getting too close to him so he pulled his arm away.

"Tell me more?" She scooted next to him.

"What are you doing?" He was confused. "Why are you pretending to care?"

"Because I do. You must feel so alone?" She rest her hand on his cheek and looked deep into his eyes. "Let Jase and I help you."

His eyes changed. The turned red and she knew that she was in trouble. She jumped and hit her head on the headboard.

Ethan saw the fear in her eyes and he turned and quickly left
the room pulling the dead stranger's body out with him.

Jase, Michael, Jessica, Rebecca, and Anthony were on their
way to Ethan's. It was starting to get dark and they knew that
they had to move fast. Anthony was fiddling around with the
windows and distracting Jase from driving.

"Anthony? Please don't do that." Jase asked kindly.

"You can't tell me what to do. You aren't my father."
Anthony refused to listen.

Jessica grabbed his hands and held them down on his lap.
"Be respectful and listen to Jase."

Anthony pulled his hands from her and spit in her face.
Jessica wiped her face and smacked him across his face. "You
will have respect."

Anthony covered his face in his hands and cried. Rebecca
leaned over and made sure that he was ok when she heard
him start chucking. "Anthony? Are you ok?" She wondered.

He didn't respond. He just continued laughing and hiding his
face.

"Anthony? Are you ok? Answer me." Rebecca demanded.

Anthony slowly took his hands down and revealed his face.
His eyes were glowing red and his fangs were present. He was
a vampire. Jase pulled the car over and Anthony leaped
across the seat to Jessica and tried biting her. She screamed
and put up a fight.

"He is a vampire!" Michael hollered as he got out of the car.

Jase pulled the back door open and grabbed Anthony from
the car and put his back against the hood.

Rebecca ran around the other side of the car. "Don't hurt
him! He is just a child!" She tried reasoning with them.

Jase continued to hold Anthony still. "Tell me what you
want!" He hollered.

"Just because you look like my father doesn't mean that I
have to answer to you." Anthony kicked at him and tried to
snap his jaw towards Jase's face.

Jase pushed him even harder. "What do you mean that I look like your father? Is Ethan your father?"

Anthony laughed some more and nodded yes. "And he is going to be so mad when he finds out that you hurt his child."

Rebecca looked at Jase and Anthony. She knew that she had to calm everyone down. "Jase, let him go."

"I can't! He is a monster!" Jase shook the little brat.

"Jase! So are you!"

The words cut through him like a knife. He knew that she was right, but he couldn't just let him go.

"We can put him in the trunk. We really don't need him to help find Ethan. By now we have to be getting close." Michael looked around at the large empty field that surrounded them. "There isn't much out this way."

Jase agreed. He grabbed Anthony and put him in the trunk as Anthony continued screaming and trying to bite. "Rebecca and Jessica, you two need to get up front. If for some reason he breaks out through the back, you are the only humans here. We are more of a fighting chance to get out alive with us being back here.

# Chapter 13

Ethan walks around his home making sure that he has no unexpected guests showing up. He had big plans for tonight and he refuses to let anyone get in his way. He was beginning to develop feelings for Katie, but he knew that she would always be faithful to Jase. He knew he had to put a stop to that and he knew that he could change her mind if he just had enough time, plus now he has Sadie as well. They could be one big happy family. He wasn't always a monster. At one time, he did know how to love, but then life got in the way and he had been hurt in so many ways, but so many people.

Ethan decided that he would check in on Sadie. She had still been unconscious from him draining her of most of her blood. He walked over to her and gave her a gentle shake. "Wake up Sadie."

She slowly opened her eyes and tried to focus on who she was seeing. She felt a little worried when she realized that it was Ethan. She grabbed her mouth, feeling for fangs, but she didn't feel anything. She grabbed her neck where he had bitten her. She was healed. Was she dreaming about this?

Ethan laughed. "Relax, I have to bite you one more time to make it official."

She was having second thoughts. She was in love with Michael but did she want to become a vampire and drink human blood. She was torn up. She loves Michael, but she had a husband and a daughter that needed her.

"I don't want to do this. I wasn't thinking clearly." She admitted with tears in her eyes.

He sat still with a smile on his face. "I understand. It isn't for everyone and I will not turn you into something you are not ready for."

She was unsure if he was being honest with her. Why would he be so nice after all of this time after everything he had done to Jase and Katie? "You're going to just let me go?"

"Of course... Believe it or not, I have nothing against you and Katie. My problem is with Jase and Rebecca." He tucked a strand of her hair behind her neck. "You are free to leave."

She slowly got out of bed. "What about Katie?"

He stood before her and gave her a sympathetic look. "She left last night. I am sure she has found Jase by now."

"How do I know that you are not lying?"

"I guess you don't, but you have my permission to look around."

Sadie walked to the door and began to open it and had a piercing pain shoot through her neck. At first, she didn't even have time to realize that Ethan had bit into her neck. She couldn't scream or cry out for help. It was like she had become paralyzed. She fell into his arms as he finished drinking from her vein and placed her on the bed.

He pulled away from her, with blood dripping from his fangs. "Sleep tight, when you awaken you will be thirsty for blood. I have a little snack waiting on you." He licked the last drop of blood from her neck and walked out leaving her lying unconscious on the bed.

Jase had fallen asleep in the backseat as they continued their search for Katie and Sadie. He began to dream and it felt real. He could see Katie and the house where she was being kept. He could see her laying in a bed. She didn't look harmed, but she was frightened. He called out to her, but she couldn't hear him. Something in his gut was leading him to her. He opened his eyes. "You're going the wrong way!" He hollered out.

Rebecca swerved and drove off the side of the road. She brought the car to a stop. "My God, Jase! You scare the hell out of me!"

Jessica and Michael looked at him. He was pale and needed blood.  "We need to get you some blood." Michael got out of the car.

"It's in the trunk with Anthony." Rebecca pointed behind her.

"Be careful," Jessica asked of him.

Michael slowly lifted the trunk to find that Anthony had drank every drop of blood. "Son of a Bitch!" Michael slammed the trunk shut.

"What's wrong?" Jessica hopped out of the car and walked over to Michael.

"He drank all of the blood. Jase and I need blood soon or we will perish. We cannot survive long without it."

"We have to look for a hospital." Jessica ran over to Rebecca and explained what was going on.

"No! There isn't enough time. Jase is already pale. If he doesn't get blood now, he won't last another hour." Michael informed them.

Rebecca looked back at her brother. She could see how weak he was and that he was fading fast.  She had an idea that she was sure might become dangerous, but she was not about to lose her brother. "You both can drink from us. We are human and if you drink from us then you will be ok."

"What? No way..."Michael refused as he pushed Jessica away.

Rebecca got out of the car and took Jase by his arm and pulled him towards her. "Jase, I know that you can do this. You would never hurt me." She cut her arm with a knife she had in her back pocket.

Jase fought back for a moment, but gave in and began drinking from her vein.

"Michael, you will die and then no one will save Sadie. She needs you to be the one who saves her." Jessica pulled her hair behind her ear exposing the artery in her neck.

He caved and began sucking her neck. It wasn't long and both men stopped nursing from their veins.

Rebecca was weak, but she would be ok once she ate something light. She grabbed a candy bar from her bag and cut it in half for Jessica.

Jessica pushed it away from her. "I don't need that."

"You have to eat. You just lost a lot of blood." Rebecca insisted.

"You don't understand. This is the second time that I have been bitten. In a little while, I will become one of them."

Rebecca was confused. The guys had only drank from them once.

"She's right." Jase interrupted. "I had drained her of blood when I got free. Remember, Rebecca. If you are bitten twice, you become one."

Rebecca's face grew long with worry. She had forgotten all about the rules of being a vampire. She could see the fear in Jessica's eyes.

"So how long do I have before it begins?" Jessica was unsure and needed answers.

Michael and Jase had no idea. Michael came back from the literal dead and Jase was unconscious at the time of his turning. "All I know is that you have to drink blood to complete it," Jase answered.

"And if I don't?" Her voice trembled.

Michael sighed. "Then you die."

Jessica's eyes filled with tears. She tried to fight them back, but she couldn't. There was so much that she had to make up for and she had to let Katie know how sorry she is.

Rebecca pulled her into a friendly embrace to offer her some comfort. "We will figure this out."

It came to Jase's attention that Anthony had been rather quiet. He hadn't heard a peep from him and Michael didn't seem to have to fight him when he tried to get the blood. "Is Anthony alright?"

"Yeah, he was fast asleep. Jase, we have to hurry up and find our women. I am afraid that we may not have much time left and it could already be too late." Michael was fearful.

"My dream was telling me where they are. I could see every detail. I saw the bed that Katie was in. She was fine. I think my dream is leading me to them."

"Well, what are we waiting for? Let's follow the broken road." Michael made a small joke to try and hide the worry on his face.

They got in the car and headed off to find the ladies again. This time they knew that they would be found. No sooner than they drove off, Anthony was awake and slammed the hood of the trunk open. They pulled over and ran around the sides of the car and caught him running through the woods.

"We have to follow him! He is going to lead us straight to Ethan!" Jase took off.

Michael, Jessica, and Rebecca followed behind him leaving the car parked on the side of the road. It was hard to see anything in the woods. Trees were everywhere and it was creepy.

"Rebecca stay close. You are now surrounded by vampires and one of them is trying to kill us." Jase encouraged her.

"Brother? I will be fine. I am just as tough as you guys." She blurted out trying to catch her breath.

They could hear Anthony giggling through the echo of the woods. He sounded so evil and crazy. He was fast, but so were most of them. Michael and Jase could smell his scent so they knew they he was not far in front of them, but he was small enough to hide anywhere.

"Come and find me if you can." Anthony chuckled.

"Anthony, we do not want to hurt anyone! We just want Katie and Sadie back!" Jase hollered.

"Katie is going to be my mom now and my dad will not let you have her back."

Jase was furious. He punch a tree that was beside him, causing it to fall over.

Rebecca could not believe how strong her brother was. She had never seen anything like it before.

"All you have to do is find me." Anthony chuckled again.

"This isn't a fucking game!" Michael was now growing angry with the little spawn of Satan.

Jessica tried to calm everyone down. "Remember, he is just a child. We have to remain calm."

"She's right." Rebecca agreed with her. "Being angry will not help us get them back. If he keeps talking we can follow the sound of his voice. It will lead us straight to them."

Jase and Michael calmed themselves down. Jessica doubled over in pain. Her stomach is in knots and she felt hungrier than she had ever been in her entire life.

Jase grabbed her, helping to steady her balance. "Are you ok?"

"I think the transformation is beginning." She explained as she held her stomach.

Michael worried. "What do we do? We can't find her blood out here?"

"She will have to feed off of me. I am the only human left." Rebecca offered her vein.

Jase grabbed Rebecca and pulled her away from Jessica. "Absolutely not! You are not giving up your humanity."

Rebecca was stubborn and refused to listen to her brother. "Jase? I will be ok. I have to do this so that she has a chance to make things right with Katie."

"Rebecca, no... You can't do this." He begged.

"Jase? I have to." She walked over to Jessica and showed her neck to her.

Jessica shook her head. "I can't do this." She cried.

"You have to or you will die." Rebecca took her by the hand and pulled her closer.

"I'm sorry," Jessica said as she pressed her lips to Rebecca's neck.

Jase couldn't watch. He turned his face away as a tear rolled down his cheek.

Michael continued watching to make sure that Jessica knew when enough was enough. He watched as Rebecca's body went limp and he ran over and pulled Jessica off of her. Jessica's eyes were bloodshot and angry-looking. She didn't want to stop.

"Jessica enough! She can't take anymore! You will kill her!" Michael demanded.

When Jase heard that Jessica wouldn't stop, he darted towards her and slung her against a tree. "Enough! If you don't want to die tonight, you will stop!"

Jessica took a few deep breaths. She looked over at Rebecca and somehow snapped herself out of it. "I am so sorry." She wiped her lips.

Michael lifted Rebecca's lifeless body in his arms. "Come on, we need to go because when she wakes up, she will need blood and right now, we don't know where to find any."

They continued listening to Anthony laughing in the woods. He sounded so far away, but they knew they were on the right path to finding the women.

Katie climbed out of the bed and ran to the door and began banging on it. "Ethan! Let me out of here!" She demanded.

Ethan walked in and walked towards her until her back was firmly pressed against the wall. His chest touched hers and he caressed her cheek with his thumb. She turned her face away from him and he pulled it back. "You will obey me."

"I will never obey you!" She hollered out.

He smiled. "You are a spitfire. I like that about you."

She tried to remain calm, but his touch sickened her. "Ethan, please just let me go. You don't have to be like this. We can all help you."

He turned around and walked away from her, but then turned to face her. "No one can help someone that doesn't want to be helped. If you knew the whole truth to why I am this way, you would understand."

"Then enlighten me. Help me understand."

He sat at the foot of the bed and stared at her for a moment, before dropping his gaze to the floor. "Did Jase ever talk about me?"

Her chest tightened. "No, I never knew he had a twin."

"Don't you think it is odd that he would never mention me?"

"There has to be a reason for it." He began to walk over towards him.

He shot a look at her. "What are you doing?"

"I was coming over to sit with you. Is that ok?"

"Why would you want to sit next to me? Aren't you scared that I might attack you?"

"I don't think you will. In fact, I don't believe that you are as bad as you want everyone to believe. I just think that you are hurt and need a friend." She sat beside him.

He could hear her heart beating in her chest. It was calm, which meant she was calm. Her eyes looked sympathetic and trusting. She wanted to understand and to be there for him. "You should have been mine. I deserve you more than Jase. I would never lie to you."

She stiffened but composed herself. She was in love with Jase and no one could ever take his place. She wasn't sure why he kept such a secret from her, but there had to be a good reason for it. "Listen, I am sure that if I had met you first that there could have been something between us, but I am in love with your brother and..."

She was interrupted. He did not want to hear any more from her. He just left the room without another word.

She leaped out of the bed and ran to the door. He left it unlocked. Was it a trick? Or did he mean to leave it open? She slowly left the room, being sure that no one spotted her. She heard noises that sounded like a woman crying from another room.  Was someone else here? Was he holding another woman hostage? She followed the sound of the weeping lady until she found the room. She went to open the door and Ethan grabbed her by the hand.

"You just can't leave well enough alone and for that, you will have to pay." He grabbed her by the throat and held her against the wall.

She could breathe and she was fighting to break free. Her legs dangled from the flood and she grabbed his hands trying to pull them off of her.

"I didn't want to hurt you, but you won't stop meddling in my plans. Now I have no choice but to kill you!"

Katie reached and clawed his face as she pushed him away. He just laughed as his skin repaired itself right in front of her. She was beginning to blackout.

Ethan heard noises coming from outside and he loosened his grip and put her back in the room where he held her hostage in. He made sure to lock the door behind him this time.

Jase, Michael, Jessica, and a passed-out Rebecca had come across a creepy victorian style house in the woods. It was dark and weary and screamed home a vampire. Michael placed Rebecca on the ground softly. "She should be ok out here for now, while we take a look around."

"We have to be careful," Jase whispered. "He can hear everything and his sense of smell is strong. He will know we are here."

"What if it finds Rebecca laying here? We can't just leave her here." Jessica worried for her.

"We have no choice. She will slow us down if we have to carry her." Michael acknowledged.

"He is right. It could be too risky. We have to make sure that he doesn't know we are here." Jase explained once more.

Michael looked up when he felt a presence staring at them from the side of the house. Ethan was standing there leaning against the house with his arms folded across his chest a smile on his face.

"Uh, guys? I think he already knows." Michael brought their attention to Ethan.

Jase and Jessica looked over and spotted Ethan watching them.

"Welcome..." Ethan giggled under his breath.

# Chapter 14

"Where are they?" Michael darted towards Ethan in anger and rage.

"Don't move!" Ethan commanded.

Michael was unable to move. Jase ran over to Michael to make sure that he was alright. "Let him go!"

"I will just ask soon as I am out of here. I guess he forgot that I control everything he does, just like I can control you as well." He smiled and then noticed that Rebecca was passed out on the ground. "I am guessing you turned our sister.

"It wasn't me. I would never hurt my sister."

"It was me and it was only to keep me from dying," Jessica admitted. "I didn't mean to turn her, but she insisted."

Ethan began to clap. "This just keeps getting better and better. Before long we will all be monsters."

"I will never be anything like you," Jase promised.

"But aren't you already? I mean we look exactly alike. Your own wife couldn't even tell the difference as I fingered her. She wanted so much more, but we were interrupted."

"You son of a Bitch!" Jase went running, but Jessica stopped him.

"Don't do anything foolish. We have to get Katie and Sadie out of here."

"I can still smell her scent on my fingers." Ethan brought his hand to his nose and began to sniff.

Jessica could see Jase clenching his fist. "He is just toying with you. Be stronger for Katie."

Jase remained calm. He took a deep breath and exhaled. "Where is she?"

"She is safe and sound in my bedroom. She is free to go whenever she would like, but she has chosen to stay."

"You are lying. She would never choose you over her children and me."

"Maybe the old her, but she is a different person now. She is one of us."

Jase gasped in horror. He did not want this life for Katie. She has two children that need her to remain human.

"I demand to see her! Right now!" Jase was angry. He wanted to kill Ethan now, but he knew that he couldn't.

"Sure, follow me. Michael, you are free to follow him." Ethan led the way into the house.

When they got inside, Anthony was sitting on the couch feeding off the man that Ethan had killed earlier that day. They looked around and didn't see the ladies anywhere and it was quiet.

"Anthony told me that you were very good to him." Ethan joked.

"I see he is following in your footsteps." Michael sneered.

"Ethan, just tell us where my daughter and her friend are. We don't want any trouble." Jessica asked.

He smiled once more. "Sure... I will take you to them, but only if you promise that you will leave in peace. I don't want to keep fighting with you guys. After all, we are family."

They all knew that he could not be trusted and that he was up to something, but they agreed and followed up the stairs. Ethan turned to face Anthony. "Anthony stay there and be good. Make sure no one enters this house."

"Yes, Father." Anthony giggled.

Jase could begin to smell Katie's scent the closer he got to the room. He was unsure of what to expect once he got there. If Ethan had turned her, she might feel differently towards him. Ethan slowly opened a door to a room and had the three of them enter. It appeared that Katie was lying in the bed under the covers and was passed out because she was not moving. Jase ran to her and gave her a gentle shake. "Katie, wake up beautiful."

The covers came down and instead of seeing Katie, it was just a dummy. Jase turned to see Ethan shutting the door. Michael ran to the door and it was locked. The doors were too hard to break through.

"I knew something felt off, but I can smell Katie. I think he had her in this room." Jase announced.

"How will we get out of here. If we don't hurry, he will turn them." Michael worried.

"There has to be a way. He had me working for him for several years and one thing I have learned is that there is always a secret way in and out of these places. That is how we were always able to escape so easily." Jessica gave them some good information.

"Then we need to begin looking for the way out before it is too late." Michael began feeling the walls.

Jase and Jessica joined in hoping that one of them would find the solution sooner than later.

Ethan had gone into a hidden area, where he kept Sadie tucked away safely. She was crouched down in a corner with sweat seeping through her pores and her eyes were glowing blue with a hint of red. She was scared and she was so hungry and she knew that she was turning into a vampire. Ethan walked over to her and grabbed her by the arm, yanking her up from the floor.

"Don't hurt me!" She cried.

He just laughed. "Why would I hurt you? I have big plans for you and right now, you need to feed."

She began to have second thoughts. She didn't want to kill anyone so that she could live.

"I have a tasty treat for you." He informed her as he walked over to a secret door that was in the room where he was keeping her.

"Wait! I can't do this! I change my mind."

He walked back over to her and pushed a curl behind her ear. "But it is too late. You are already one of us and believe me, I got something tasty for you. You are going to love this."

Ethan walked back over to the secret room. "Come to me."

Sadie did as was commanded of her. She had no control over her own choices anymore. She was under his compulsion.

They entered the secret room and as they go further in, she saw Katie sitting tied up to a chair with a gag in her mouth and a blindfold over her eyes.

"Remain quiet." He whispered. "There is more."

All she could think is that she was about to be forced to kill her best friend and she could not do that. She had to somehow break free from his control.

Ethan pulled a curtain open to a closet that he had Jackson and Anna in. Sadie's eyes widened and her heartbeat sped up. A tear fell from her eye.

Ethan walked over to her and began to massage her shoulders as he leaned in and whispered into her right ear. "Are you hungry?"

She nodded her head yes.

"Good girl." He licked the side of her cheek.

She pulled her face away in disgust.

Ethan took her by the hand and walked her over to Jackson. "I will let you choose because I am not a monster. You can either drain Jackson of all of his blood or..." He paused for a moment. "You can kill your daughter."

She began to cry because she knew that she had to do whatever he asked her to do. She was not strong enough to fight back. She shook her head no as the tears fell from her eyes.

Ethan pulled her closer. "My dear... You do not have any other choice. You must decide if you love Jackson more than your daughter. Personally, I would kill him. He seems like a jerk."

"Sadie?" Katie called out. "Don't listen to him!"

Sadie turned her head towards Katie, who had managed to get the gag out of her mouth.

Ethan quickly went over to her and placed the gag back into her mouth while she struggled to fight him. He rubbed her head as though she was a pet of his. Sadie wanted to scream out but she could not make a sound.

Jackson finally came to and saw Sadie standing in front of him. "Sadie? Where am I? What's going on?" He questioned.

Sadie stared at him without being able to speak. Tears were still falling from her eyes. "Please run away Jackson." She thought to herself.

"Sadie? Answer me... What the hell is going on and how did I get here?"

Ethan walked over and knelt down on the floor in front of Jackson. "That's right. You don't know what is going on."

"Jase what the hell are you talking about?" Jackson tried to break free from the chair.

Ethan grabbed him by the face. "My name is Ethan. Jase is my twin brother."

Jackson was confused. He didn't know that Jase had a twin. "Sadie? Why aren't you saying anything?"

"Oh yeah, she is under my compulsion. You see, I am a vampire and soon once she drinks from your vein, she will also be one."

"What?" He looked up at Sadie who was just standing there.

Ethan stood up and looked at Sadie. "Go ahead and show him the monster that you are."

Without even trying her eyes began to glow and her fangs showed.

Jackson was mortified. He couldn't even speak as his mind began spinning.

"You can speak again," Ethan whispered into her ear.

"Jackson, please get our baby and run." She begged.

"But how can he run? He is tied down and too weak to fight against us."

"I won't let you hurt him." She promised.

"I know, but you will. You have no choice. You either kill Jackson, or you kill your baby." Ethan ordered.

"Please don't make me do this." She pleaded.

"You do as I say. There is no other choice."

"But they are my family. Anna is just a baby."

"I don't care. Choose now!" He demanded.

She struggled as tears continued falling from her eyes.

"Sadie look at me," Jackson asked. "Choose me. Save Anna, she is just a baby. It is ok." He offered himself up.

"I can't control myself. He is controlling me." She slowly walked over to him and faced him.

"It's ok." He stated.

"I'm so sorry." She opened her mouth and went to bite his neck, but was grabbed from behind.

Rebecca had barged in and pulled Sadie away from Jackson. "No! I won't let you do this!"

Ethan turned around and just laughed at his sister. "Well done, Sis... I am impressed, but not too much because you are not strong enough to fight a vampire. You haven't drunk blood yet."

Rebecca stood in front of Jackson, keeping him safe from Sadie. "Haven't I? While you were in here playing games and disrupting everyone's lives, I killed a deer in the woods. You see, I too can be a monster just like you, when it comes to saving the people that I love."

Ethan grew frustrated with Rebecca. How dare she spoil his plan to have Sadie kill her husband.

"You think you have won, but I can promise you that it has only begun. Jackson has no chance with Sadie. After all, she is in love with Michael and he is alive and already back in her bed."

Jackson heard what was said. "What the fuck are you talking about?!"

Ethan was cold-hearted. He loved causing havoc in their lives. In fact, he got off on it. "That's right. Michael is alive. He is a vampire and him and Sadie have already done the dirty. He couldn't keep his hands off of her and she didn't stop it."

"Shut up! You are lying!" Jackson tried to loosen the restraints.

Sadie didn't respond. She stayed pressed against the wall hiding her shame.

"Sadie, tell him the truth and make sure you only be honest. No sugar coating the truth." Ethan compelled her once more.

"Sadie? Is this true?" Jackson stared at her waiting to hear what she had to say.

Sadie sat down on the floor and pulled her knees to her chest.

"Sadie? Answer me." Jackson begged.

"It's all true. Michael is back and yes we made love, but you have to understand. I was in shock and when I saw him, it caught me off guard. I was so in love with him and..."Jackson interrupted her.

"Shut the fuck up! I am not sure what the hell is going on, but I am done with you and I am done with these little games that all of you are playing." He tried to rip the ropes that bound him to the chair.

Anna began to cry. She must be scared or hungry. Sadie walked over to her and went to pick her up.

"Don't you dare touch her! You are a monster and there is no way that I would ever allow someone like you to be a mother to my daughter!"

Sadie grew angry and snapped at him and Rebecca grabbed her. "You don't want to do that."

"How dare you! I have been a good mom to her. I love my daughter." Sadie defended herself.

"Yeah well now you are a blood-lusting creature and I refuse to allow you near my daughter!"

Sadie leaped over Rebecca and knocked Jackson from the chair causing the restraints to come off and he hit his head on the floor knocking him unconscious.

Rebecca grabbed Sadie and slung her across the room. "Sadie No! He is your husband and you are not thinking clearly right now!"

"No! You don't understand! Ethan has compelled me to kill Jackson or my daughter and I am choosing Jackson. I can't control this!" She swung at Rebecca and knocked her right through the wall.

Sadie grabbed a pipe that was hanging from the wall and punctured it right through Rebecca's chest. Rebecca cried out in pain and could not move.

Sadie turned to walk toward Jackson once more. She was not going to stop until he was dead and her daughter was safe. She got down on the floor and began feeding on his vein. She felt her nerves coming to life and she felt stronger than she had ever felt before.

Ethan stood back watching her drain Jackson. It thrilled him to see her devour him as though he was nothing. "He is almost dead. Keep drinking. It won't be much longer and then we can move onto the second part of my plan."

A crash came through the wall. Michael and Jase had barged in and stopped Sadie. He had blood dripping from her lips and she hissed at them. She didn't want to stop. She had to finish him off.

"Snap out of it Sadie! It's me, Michael." He tried to shake her back to her senses.

Jessica saw Rebecca lying on the ground with a pipe pierced through her and she went over to help. "This is going to hurt, but you will be able to heal once I remove it." Jessica ripped the pipe from her body and tossed it to the side.

"Enough!" Ethan hollered in fury.

Everything got quiet as they noticed that Ethan had Katie in his arms. He had her neck exposed and was ready to turn her at any moment and all it would take was one simple bite to complete it.

"Ethan? Please don't do this. Let's just talk about it. I understand that you are angry at me for some reason, but Katie has nothing to do with it." Jase walked a little closer.

"Don't you think that I know that?" He ran his hands along her arm to try and comfort her. "I don't want to hurt her. For some strange reason, I actually like her. But that doesn't change things. If I turn her, she can be mine."

Michael continued holding Sadie until she calmed down. She was still going to kill Jackson, but for now, her hunger was satisfied enough to focus on what was going on.

"Ethan? You say you like her... Then let it be her choice to change. Don't take the right from her." Jase pleaded.

"You mean like you took the choice from me?" Ethan spit out.

Jase was unsure of what he meant. What choice has he taken from him? He hadn't seen him since they were children. "What do you mean?"

"You know what I mean. Stop pretending and let everyone know exactly what kind of man you really are."

Katie was listening to everything that was being said. She was so scared, but she knew that she had to say something and try to calm Ethan down. Maybe he would listen to her.

"Ethan? Please listen to Jase... Just talk to him and try to compromise. There is no need for anyone else to get hurt." She asked of him.

Ethan paused for a moment and then let her go. She stopped and stared at Ethan instead of running towards Jase. She walked over to Ethan and tried to comfort him. "This is not your fault. Something bad happened to you as a child and you need help to heal from it. Let us help you."

"Katie? What are you doing? Come over here away from him." Jessica called out.

When Ethan heard Jessica's words he snatched Katie back into his arms and held her tight against his chest. "Everyone thinks that I am a monster, so I may as well prove you all right!" He went to bite her neck and stopped when he saw Anthony walk in.

"Dad? Don't hurt her. You said she was going to be my new mom." Anthony walked over to them.

"Anthony? This is the only way to make sure that she becomes your mom. If she stays human, she will always have free will and she will never choose you over her other kids." Ethan tightened his grip on her.

"Then let her go. I don't want a mom that doesn't want me."

"This isn't your choice," Ethan explained. "They have to pay for what they did."

"But she is innocent. Jase and Rebecca are the ones you are mad at. Shouldn't you talk to them and take it out on them?"

"You are too young to understand," Ethan admitted.

Anthony became very upset and ran off. He never could get Ethan to listen to him.

Jase worried for Katie. He had to get her somehow, but he didn't know how he could.

"Look, if you want to make me pay, fine. Take me... torture me or kill me. I don't care. Just let her go." Jase offered himself over.

Ethan let Katie go and this time she ran right into Jase's arm. He held her tight and kissed her cheek. "I've got you beautiful."

# Chapter 15

Ethan walked closer to Jase and Rebecca. Jase was sure to keep him from getting to Katie again. He made her stand behind him to protect her.

"Do you honestly not really remember what happened the night our mother died?" Ethan wondered.

"What do you mean? Of course, I do. Our father beat her to death and by the time I go to her it was too late." Jase answered.

Ethan laughed and shook his head. "Wrong... I killed our mother. It was me. I drained her of all of her blood and she deserved it."

Jase did not know why he was saying this. He remembered that night and he remember seeing his mother lying in a puddle of blood on the floor and he was too young to help.

"Rebecca was at school and I was home alone. I heard them fighting and I ran downstairs to the kitchen to help, but it was too late and our father was gone. Never to be seen or heard from again." Jase recalled.

"No brother... That is not true. I guess even has a child I was able to compel you because we shared the same blood." Ethan walked over closer and stared Jase in the eyes. "Remember that night."

All of a sudden that night came flooding back to his mind. He could see it all so clearly as though it was going on right in front of him.

He had heard a struggle but when he came downstairs to help, he had seen Ethan biting into his mother's neck and feeding on her vein. Jase had screamed out loud to make Ethan stop and when Ethan looked at him, he was a vicious monster. He had walked over to Jase and had told him to forget that he had a brother and that all he could remember was that his father was abusive and killed their mother. He would later that day tell his sister what he was made to believe and he would blame himself for years to come.

Jase gasped as the memories became too strong. He began to weep and his hands trembled. All he could find the strength to ask was "Why?"

"Our father had turned our mother into a monster and she turned me. She wanted to turn you and Rebecca as well, but I refused to let her, so I killed her. I knew that this would not be a life that you would be happy with, but then you so easily moved on and never remembered me. As a child on my own, I had hoped that you guys would remember. After all, I never compelled our sister."

"I talked about you. When Jase kept talking about that night I kept asking where you were. He told me that you didn't exist. We just thought he was in shock, so we had to show him pictures to help him remember." Rebecca informed him.

"She's telling the truth and I was about to let Katie know, but then I was in the wreck and that was when I somehow woke up with you and Jessica standing over me."

Ethan smiled. "That was so easy to do. With us being identical twins, no one suspected anything. I am just curious, knowing that you had a brother that was still alive out there somewhere, did you ever try to find me?"

"I did," Rebecca announced. "I tried several times."

"Really? Because I only tried finding you both once and here I am. I don't believe you tried hard enough."

"Ethan, I didn't try finding you. I had a hard time wrapping my mind around why you would just run off. I honestly thought you were dead. " Jase wiped his eyes.

Katie squeezed Jase's hand trying to comfort him the best that she could at this moment.

Ethan came closer to him. "I ran off so that you and Rebecca wouldn't have to live this life."

"But where is our father? If he is the one that turned our mother then where is he?" Rebecca asked.

"I don't know. He was evil so I am sure he is out there killing everyone and everything. He did not care who he hurt." Ethan replied.

"But you surely have some good in you?" Rebecca wondered.

"I use to, but after being on my own for years I learned to stop caring about stuff. You see when you become a vampire as a child, you stop aging by the time you are 35. If you are bitten as an adult, you just stay the age you are. All those years alone made me crazy with rage and all I can think about is hurting you all."

"No!" Katie spoke up. "That's not true... You have a soft side. I have seen it. You are choosing to hide it instead of letting anyone in."

Ethan looked over at Katie who was hiding behind Jase. He could see that she genuinely cared for him and wanted to be there to help, but he didn't need her or anyone else. "Do you honestly think that I would want any of you to pretend to care about me? I won't stop until you are all dead!"

Ethan's attitude changed drastically as his eyes glowed red. When Katie saw his eyes, she knew they were in trouble. Ethan leaped towards Jase, but Michael jumped in front of him, knocking him across the room. They stumbled across the room back and forth throwing punches.

Rebecca grabbed the baby and fled the scene. She knew that she had to keep the baby safe. Jackson was coming to. He was very faint and tried to get up. He could see them battling against each other. Sadie watched him struggle to get up and she knew that she still had to kill him. She had no other choice.

Katie noticed that Sadie was moving in on Jackson and she ran to her. "Sadie! NO!" Katie hollered.

Sadie stared at Katie with her eyes glowing and her fangs showing. She hissed at Katie to let her know that she needed to stay back.

"Sadie... This isn't you. You have to fight it." Katie explained.

"You don't understand. I can't. I am compelled and if I don't do it, I will die." She cried during a weak moment.

"Sadie, you can't do this. He is the father of your baby. She needs both of her parents."

"No! She is not Anna's mother anymore. She is a blood-thirsty monster and she will never come near my daughter." Jackson stated.

"Jackson, shut up!" Katie gave him a look of disgust.

"He's right... I am blood-thirsty and I will not stop until he is dead so I need you to kill me." Sadie asked of her.

Katie took a step back and her eyes swelled with tears. "What? No... I am not going to kill you."

"If you don't kill me, I will kill him and I could never live with myself knowing that I killed the father of my child. Please, Katie... You have to do this for me."

Jackson threw a part of a broken chair to Katie. "Do it! Kill her!"

Katie was furious with Jackson. How could he want Sadie dead so easily? He was no better than any of them. "I can't do it."

Sadie took the broken chair piece from Katie and pushed it through her own chest. She knew that Katie would not do it and she was running out of time. Sadie fell to her knees as tears fell from her eyes. "Tell Anna that her mother loved her very much."

"Sadie... No! You shouldn't have done that!" Katie knelt beside her and held her in her arms.

The men stopped battling when they heard Katie cry out. "Sadie!" Michael ran towards her.

Sadie was growing weaker by the minute. Michael moved Katie from her and took her place. "What did you do?" He kissed her cheek.

"She's going to be ok. Ethan told me she would have to be decapitated to die. This will just paralyze her for a bit until we take it out." Katie remembered the conversation she had with Ethan.

Michael was enraged. He snatched Jackson from the floor and slammed his back against the wall. "She deserves better than you!"

Jase quickly ran to him and pulled him back. "It isn't worth it. Let him go."

Michael slowly loosened his grip on Jackson and let him go. "Get out of here and never look back. If you so much as ever come near her, I will kill you myself." Michael threatened.

Jackson took off running trying to escape from the house. He now had to find Rebecca and get his daughter back.

Jase and Michael turned to go after Ethan once more, but when they turned around, Ethan and Katie were gone. Jessica was pinned to the wall covered in blood. "I tried to stop him, but I couldn't. He took Katie." She coughed.

Michael pulled the pins from her skin. There were so many long, thick pins in her skin.

"I can still smell them. They are not far." Jase took off running.

Jase ran so fast through the woods and he knew he was getting closer. He could smell their scents even stronger. He froze when he realized that Ethan was standing on the ledge of a cliff holding Katie by her arm.

"Ethan? Let's just talk about this. We can fix this." Jase slowly walked a little closer to them.

"Don't come any closer or I will push her off and watch her fall to her death."

"Jase! Just listen to him!" Katie cried out.

Ethan pulled Katie into a warm embrace and held her against his chest. "Shhhh... It's ok. I would never hurt you." He whispered.

"Ethan just let her go. This is between me and you. She is innocent." Jase begged as he saw the tears streaming down Katie's face.

"She has everything to do with it. You see brother, I am in love with her and she is in love with you. That is a big problem" Ethan caressed her cheek with his thumb.

Katie trembled in his arms. She was mortified and didn't know what was going to happen. "Ethan? Please..."

"It's okay baby... As long as Jase makes the right choice, everything will be ok. I promise."

Jase wasn't sure of what he meant by that. He was a little weary of Ethan's plans for them.

"You are going to love the choice that I am about to give you. It is exhilarating. I am actually pleased with how easy it was for me to come up with this." Ethan smiled.

Michael, Sadie, and Jessica met up with Jase. Jase stopped them from getting any closer.

"Oh good, the party is starting. The more the merrier." Ethan was sarcastic.

"What the hell do you want, Ethan?" Michael snapped.

"Let her go!" Sadie demanded.

Ethan laughed. "Do you really want me to let her go?" Ethan dangled Katie over the ledge.

Katie screamed out in horror. Jase panicked. "No!"

Ethan pulled Katie back into his arms. "I am just kidding. That was a good one."

"Ethan? You don't want to do this." Jessica spoke up.

He rolled his eyes. "Everyone pretends that they know what I want, but they haven't a clue."

"Then talk to us. Let us understand." Jase begged as he continued to watch Katie. Seeing her so scared was eating away at him.

"Katie? I know you can't trust me, but I want you to know that I will not let anything happen to you." Jessica promised. "I am so sorry that I have been such a terrible mother, but I was under his control this whole time."

"Mom? I understand and I forgive you, but he isn't going to hand me over unless everyone does what he wants." Katie cried out.

Ethan licked a tear from her cheek. "Aw... That was so touching. It made my heart flutter."

"Listen, take me instead. Let my daughter go and just take me."

"You forget... I have already had you and it wasn't good. Now Katie would be a spitfire in bed compared to you."

Ethan noticed that Michael had a huge knife hidden behind his back. "You know what Jessica? I am tired of hearing your voice. Michael? Take that knife and cut her head off. Kill her now." Ethan compelled Michael.

"What? NO! Michael don't listen!" Katie pleaded.

Michael couldn't control it. Jessica looked at Katie and once more before she died she was able to tell her daughter that she loved her. "I love you, Katie."

Katie sobbed and tried kicking her legs to break free. "I love you! Please, Michael!"

Michael took the knife and with one slice he took her head off. Her body fell to the ground as her head remained in Michael's hand.

"Noooo!" Katie cried. "Mom!"

Jase began to run to comfort Katie, but Ethan pulled her hair back and showed his fangs. "I will bite her and I will turn her into one of us."

Jase stopped dead in his tracks. "Don't do this! What do you want?! I will do whatever you ask. Just don't hurt her."

Ethan gave an evil smirk. "I want you to walk away from Katie and come with me to find out father. You are to stay away from Katie and never return to her or I will come back and finish you all off. This is the only way that I will let you all go."

"Jase! Please don't listen!" Katie begged.

Jase looked over at Katie and then back at Ethan. He knew that Ethan meant what he said. "If we find our father will I be free to come back to Katie?" Jase wondered.

Ethan shook his head. "No... She is never to be with you again. This is solely your choice."

"And if I choose to do this, you will let her go? All of them will be able to live normal lives and you will not compel them anymore?"

"I am a man of my word. Do this and I will uncompel everyone and it will be like none of this ever happened."

Jase thought for a moment. He could see that Katie's heart was breaking inside. "If I do this, can I tell Katie goodbye?"

Ethan nodded. "Sure... I'm not a complete monster."

"Fine, I will do it. Just let her go and I will do whatever you want me to do."

Ethan was happy. He didn't think it would be this easy to convince him. He let Katie go and she ran right into Jase's arms and held him tight. Jase kissed her several times and didn't want to let her go. "It's okay baby... This is just for now. I will find my way back to you. I promise."

"Don't leave me." She cried. "I just got you back. I need you." She tightened her grip.

"I have to go. This is the only way to keep you and our children and friends safe."

"I can't do it without you."

Jase took her face in his hands and looked deeply into her eyes. "You can do it. You are the strongest woman I have ever known." He whispered as he kissed her once more. "I love you so much, Beautiful."

"I love you too." She responded one more time before watching him go over to Ethan.

Ethan told Sadie that she was free from having to kill Jackson and he promised that he would never interfere in their lives again. He then left at lightning speed with Jase. They moved so fast that no one saw them. Katie's heart ached inside and she didn't know how she could go on without Jase, but she knew that she had to for their children.

Jackson ended up finding Rebecca and took his daughter and made sure that Sadie was never left unattended around Anna. He promised not to tell anyone that she was a vampire, but he didn't want anything to do with her anymore.

Michael and Sadie ended up trying to repair their relationship in hopes that one day, things would feel normal around them again.

Rebecca went home to live her new life as a vampire with her husband that was very much human and Katie tried to play both mom and dad for her children while pretending to be happy.

Jase never spent a day without thinking about Katie and his children. He knew that he would find his father and then he would take Ethan and his father down, once and for all. No one would stop him from being with Katie, the love of his life. He would see them again and this time, he would never let them go.